THE PSI-CHOTIC ADVENTURES OF DREW DARBY

RICHARD W. KELLY

THE PSI-CHOTIC ADVENTURES OF DREW DARBY

ISBN: 978-1-971461-02-1

TITLES BY RICHARD W. KELLY
MEENDUK.COM

Bizarro
- The Cattercorns of Cloudville Arizona

Christian
- My Journey Into Christianity
- Noel Not an Angel: A Christmas Novella

Fantasy
- Kings of One Color

Historical Fiction
- The Early Years of 'Squirt' Malone

Horror
- Testament

Short Stories
- Solundrums
- Solundrums V.2 – Mid 2025

Slice of Life Books
- The Cultural Phenomenon of Super Jam and the Tragedy Therein
- Lost Vegas, Nevada
- A Novella About Pie That Should Have Starred Jason Sudeikis
- Times... They Are A Changin'

Thriller
- The American Martyr
- The MARX Beasts – Late 2025

Young Adult
- The Psi-Chotic Adventures of Drew Darby

THANK YOU

I would like to thank Phyllis Foley for editing this manuscript. And my wife for editing all the others.

ONE

SOLITARY CONFINEMENT, PLEASE

The engine revved with humiliation as Drew steered toward his new place of employment. The bright greens and yellows of his HappyLand employees' shirt mocked his sixteen year old brain with the unwanted reality that he was who he did not want to be.

A green light released him from his neighborhood drawing him ever closer to the ridicule that was likely to accompany his first day on the new job. His foot let up on the gas and shifted over to the brake pedal of his ten year old car. He drove the decade old rusted out hatchback every day to his high school where he lugged a huge tuba in and out of the small car and into the band hall where he helped the band director police the halls and snitch on his fellow students who were breaking rules. He sported old fashioned pilot glasses that came down below his cheek bones magnifying the blemishes on his face. He even let his hair hang shaggy and in need of a trim while leaving a receding hairline already noticeable at his young age. All these things and being employed by HappyLand left his stomach twisting with anticipation of the humility.

He drove his beloved vehicle into a left turn lane and stared out the side window at the hideous fast food restaurant that matched his bright shirt glowing from the corners of his vision. The light flashed a green arrow. He stared at the building. The arrow turned yellow, then red. Honks came from behind him upset that he refused to go to work. A deep breath filled Drew's lungs and he turned back to the traffic light.

His eyes trained on the red circle, but the cartoon colored restaurant mocked him from the periphery. When the green arrow came back Drew forced himself to press the gas pedal just enough to approach the store. Dark music played in his head as he slowly crept toward HappyLand. The soundtrack in his mind could have been appropriate for an approaching army of demons, but that would somehow seem less intimidating than the idea of being seen working for HappyLand.

Still barely rolling down the road, his car gently drove up the driveway into the parking lot. He instinctively parked in the back and let his head fall into his hands as he overdramatized his unfortunate place of employment.

His stomach filled with the uncomfortable carbonation of anticipation as he opened the car door and placed his black sneakers on the asphalt. Every step he took toward the door felt like a step toward the end of his social life or at least what was left of it. As the wind played with his unkempt hair he scorned his parents for forcing him to take a job.

They saw his lack of friends as a weakness and making him gain employment was their only solution. His pleas for a reprieve fell on deaf ears when his father called an old buddy who happened to own a franchise of the horrid HappyLand outside their neighborhood.

Drew had told them he was fine, that he did not need money, that many highly looked upon people were hermits, but it was no use. Apparently, his parents did not want to raise a monk or a serial killer and chained him to the prison that was a job.

Drew looked at the door not wanting to walk inside. It was a metaphor for an entry into a darker world. Or maybe it was an exit from his childhood. Either way he did not want to enter. He could see Mr. Harkins walking around with perfect posture in his sweat-stained Wal-Mart business attire. The pale blue tie swung around his thick neck reminding Drew that his new boss and his father's longtime friend was former military. The realization of just how horrifying his new militaristically disciplined career may be caused his knees to go weak.

Drew's balance went and he fell forward with his face and the glass echoing an ugly splat into the dining room. This caught the ear of Mr. Harkins who quickly trotted over to obtain his new employee.

The manager's military humor kicked in as he pushed the door open with enough force to toss Drew into the parking lot while he remarked, "Oh, gee, didn't see ya there young man."

Drew pulled himself to his feet refusing to look Mr. Harkins in the eye. He walked with slunk shoulders past his new boss and into the headache-igniting dining room of HappyLand. The bright greens and yellows made Drew squint in agony, a feeling he never felt as a customer in the grease-filled death trap.

Mr. Harkins looked down on the boy, slightly disgusted with his lack of self-hygiene or at least self-respect for his fashion sense. "Report to the training room behind the kitchen. You are a bit early, sit in a chair and wait for your trainer to arrive." He turned on his heel to march back to the bathrooms leaving Drew to find the training room on his own.

He watched the ground as he walked past the cashier's counter and into the kitchen. Slipping on the greasy floor he kept his eyes on the ground to avoid meeting a gaze with anyone who was employed there. He knew that he was on the low end of the high school totem pole, but that did not mean he did not want to move up on that scale and working at HappyLand could do nothing but the opposite.

A deep voice came from Drew's right directing him to the training room which he mechanically wandered into. The floor went from a greasy slip and slide to dry rubber tiles being temporarily tarnished by his now filthy black sneakers. The room was very empty - a chair, a television and a few inspirational posters on the wall. Drew collapsed into the chair, exasperated with defeat.

He looked at the walls ready to give in and accept the misery that was now to be his life. He read the first inspirational poster trying to convince his sub-conscience to learn its lesson.

The first in the nice line of six inspirationals said, "Get up and get to work, NOW." Drew thought to himself, 'I don't feel motivated.' The accompanying picture was no help either, just an empty boat with a paddle lying inside.

The next said, "The job you deserve is this one." The picture was a smiling cartoon sheep knitting a sweater. Another feeling of self-worthlessness swept over him.

"Hell isn't punishment, it's just for failures." Above the slogan was a picture of an ugly bodybuilder type man that had so much of a fake tan that he looked orange. In it he was signing a last will and testament and he was oddly happy about it. Drew could not stop his disgust at how demented Mr. Harkins was.

"Out of desperation, unwavering dedication is born." This one had a picture of a man from the eyes up tapping his temple as if to say, "What an epiphany this is." There was an odd tattoo on the man's hand, looking somewhat like the Greek letter 'delta'.

"Of everything you want, you have this." Mr. Harkins was pictured above the somewhat inspirational line in full military garb with a very serious look on his face, but for some reason he had one eye opened wide while the other was noticeably closed.

Drew thought how much his new boss had fallen

from the height of the military to being a lowly fast food manager.

The last poster bore the image of two people on a roller coaster with a thought bubble above their heads saying "YipeeeeeE!" The last e in the word was oddly capitalized. Drew wondered about the purpose of the capitalization as he read the line below. "Here is the rest of your life."

He leaned back in the chair looking at the line of posters, the big E in the last still perplexing him. Out of boredom he started to play with the posters, counting the number of words in each phrase, looking for repeating words, comparing the background colors of each…

But after a couple of coincidences, he noticed something that made his neck hair stand on end. The first word of each poster made a sentence he did not want to see. "Get the Hell out of here." He figured it to be coincidence, but it made him a bit nervous.

Unable to sit still he continued searching the signs for other hidden messages. He kept staring at the E.

He looked at the 'delta' in the fourth picture and couldn't help but focus on Mr. Harkins' eye in the fifth. His heart began to race as he put the letters together. Delta was the Greek letter for D. Eye. E. DIE. Drew's breathing began to pound his chest. His heart was racing faster than he could handle.

The rest of the posters began to make sense. There was an oar in the boat. A female sheep was a ewe. The orange man was signing a will. He put them all together. Oar ewe will

D I E. Get the Hell out of here or you will die.

Drew was terrified. Forget coincidence he decided as he sprang toward the door realizing there was no handle on the inside. The message made no sense, there was no reason for him to fear for his life, but it was no time for logic.

Drew took a few steps back into the room and charged the door with a shoulder block. He bounced off the steel door and fell to the ground, his head cracking against a hard rubber tile dislodging it from the ground. He picked up the tile instinctively wanting to return it to its place when he noticed the word wrong was written on the back of it accompanied by a small twenty-seven. He turned to his side and ripped up the tile next to it.

Another wrong with the number twenty-six. Over the intercom came a weasel-y little voice speaking directly to Drew. "I'll be in a minute, why don't you turn on the TV before we get started."

Drew tried to ignore his fears and turned on the television, telling himself he was crazy. The old television came on with a small electrical buzz in the background.

There was a man in a HappyLand hat talking about inspiration, but Drew could not focus. He kept looking at the tiles on the ground that he had pulled up. There were eight tiles from wall to wall in each direction making sixty-four tiles total. Counting from the front corner of the room they were tiles number fourteen and fifteen. Counting from another direction they were tiles ten and eighteen. Why were they labeled twenty-six and twenty-seven?

The television spoke in the background, "At HappyLand we help every customer. We pay attention to every word. If we are speaking to a customer, we count every smile. If we are cleaning, we clean every tile. If we are reporting, we pay attention to every column and every row. "

Drew continued to try to calm himself down by taking slow relaxed breaths while the television repeated the same line over and over. As his heart rate slowed, the words of the TV drilled into his skull as if he was having brain surgery. He began to chant the line.

"Every word", he paused. "Every Smile", another pause. "Every column, every row", then it hit him. The tile was not labeled twenty-seven it was column two row seven. His connection to the randomness of the situation pumped the adrenaline back into his veins.

He repeated things to himself again. Word. Smile. Column. Row. He turned back to the poster and counted words again. Forty-two. That can't be it. Six posters and each had seven words. So, seven was the column. He looked back at the posters looking for smiles. The sheep was smiling, the orange man, and the two coaster riders. Four.

He kicked the chair out of the way to get to tile seven four. Again fearing for his life, he pawed at the rubber square yanking it out of the ground. As the tile came up, he could see a small red button sunken into the ground. Without hesitation he pressed the plastic circle and the door popped open.

A wave of relief flushed through Drew's body as he

saw his freedom open to the kitchen. Until he saw Mr. Harkins step into the door frame. The large fit man stepped into the room closing the door behind him.

"Let me out of here! My dad knows where I am!" Drew screamed out through the crackling in his pubescent voice. His hand kept mashing the red button popping the door back open.

Mr. Harkins kept slamming the door each time it popped open. His jaw began to clench and his face reddened. "Drew. Stop hitting that button. NOW!"

"I don't know why you want to kill me, but…"

"I am not going to kill you." He took a step toward Drew, but had to retreat to close the door again. "I said stop it."

Drew just kept pressing the button as tears weld up in his eyes.

"You are safe. I need your help actually."

"What are you talking about?" The words came out in globs past the tears streaming down the boys cheeks.

"Pull yourself together! You are the first one to solve the puzzle. You are only the second one to notice it even exists."

This caught Drew off guard. Maybe he was safe after all. "Puzzle?"

"Yes, it is just a puzzle. We need to be able to identify those who can read between the lines of the universe."

Drew popped the door again. He was relaxing a bit, but still didn't trust Mr. Harkins. "Who is we?"

Richard W. Kelly

"The United States military."

TWO

APRIL MAKES YOU WONDER IF YOU WANT TO JOIN

Drew sat inside another stark white room. This time there were no posters to encourage inspiration. Instead he was left to take the ASVAB, otherwise known as the Armed Services Vocational Aptitude Battery. There was a camera in the ceiling watching him, making sure he was being honest in his test taking tactics.

His hand shook as he filled in the bubbles on the sheet. The graphite of the pencil smeared outside the small circles while his body refused to leave the fight or flight mode. Drew worried that he may not be delivering his best work since he was so shaken up, but even in a traumatized form his agile mind was no match for the ASVAB.

He breezed through the math portions, the grammar, and the vocabulary. He answered them so quickly that when he stood up to signal his completion of the test a voice boomed over the intercom. "Why don't you take another look at those answers, son. This could change your life."

Drew slowly bent his legs and returned to his seat. The rough fabric of the cheap chair irritated his back, but hearing someone suggest he missed something focused him. The lack of decoration in the room became a non-issue. The annoyance of the uncomfortable chair dissipated into a void. The hideousness of his eyesore of a shirt left his mind. Even the excitement of the events earlier were forgotten. Now he was determined to ace the test that lay in front of him.

He began by going back through the questions themselves, but he made quick work of that review. Then he began to check the patterns of his answers. A. B. A. C. D. C. B. A. D. D. D. A. B. D. A. He saw no discernable patterns. He flipped through the pages looking at the wording of each question searching for some hidden code that may give him instructions on what else to do on the test. Nothing.

He began to look around the room, but it was blank. His mind raced with possible patterns he could look for, but every one that he investigated turned out to be a dead end. He put his hand on his forehead trying to force back an impending headache knowing that the action was futile. He was exhausted mentally and still no answers as to why he needed to look again at the test.

He hunched down in the chair and asked himself why he cared so much. Why did he want to perform well on a military aptitude test? He had no desire to join the military. He was still in high school. He couldn't enlist until he was eighteen anyway.

The door smashed into the wall and Mr. Harkins

stood on the threshold. "I assume you are done." He stretched his arm out toward Drew awaiting the test.

"Sure." Drew was beaten down and defeated. It didn't matter anymore to him if he passed or not. His head facing the blank table he blindly handed the test over to his boss.

"Good. I will return with your results shortly." Mr. Harkins was out the door before Drew could make any inquiries. But there was not a long wait in the room before Mr. Harkins was back in the doorway along with two other men in what appeared to be some sort of uniform.

There was a black man and a white man, both with the short crew cuts and both were standing straight up with their hands behind their backs. Their clothes reminded drew of Star Trek. Black skin tight pants with what appeared to be a spandex shirt coming out of the top. They also both adorned a single badge portraying an unfinished pyramid with the eye of providence above it, the same symbol that was on the back of the United States one dollar bill.

The three men stepped into the room and closed the door behind them. The sight brought fear into the heart of Drew as his knees quaked even while sitting in the chair. He took a hard swallow and tried to compose himself.

"Mr. Darby?" Mr. Harkins waited for Drew to answer, but the association he had with his father and the name Mr. Darby left him quiet. "Drew?"

The boy looked up into the eyes of Mr. Harkins.

"Stand up, boy." Mr. Harkins voice went soft as if not

to tip off the other two men that Drew did not understand. "I need you to raise your right hand, repeat after me."

"What? I haven't agreed to anything! I can't join the military; I'm not even old enough." Drew went right back into panic mode.

"Major Smith here has your new documents. You are now eighteen."

The black man stepped forward and placed a new social security card, driver's license, and birth certificate on the table. Lesson one - the government can solve a simple problem like age.

"No! I am in high school. I have my parents here. I can't just up and leave and join…"

Mr. Harkins cut him off. "Drew." Mr. Harkins abandoned his authoritative tone. "You don't understand what is being offered to you. This is your chance to be a hero. This is your chance to make a difference. This is not just military service; this is saving mankind from evil."

"But…what about my life here? What about my friends?" He was lying. He didn't have any friends. "What about my family?"

"All will be taken care of. And you will only be gone in short bursts. If you pass this up, you will be missing out on a whole different world. If you walk out of this building without us, you will just be a HappyLand cashier."

That was the motivation Drew needed. He had not put two and two together. Joining Mr. Harkins was his out. It was his relief from the torment of high school, from the embarrassment of HappyLand. He stood up and raised his right hand.

"I, Drew Darby." Mr. Harkins reverted back to his military voice.

"I Drew Darby."

"Do solemnly swear"

"Do solemnly swear"

"That I will support and defend the constitution of the United States against all enemies foreign and domestic." Drew repeated. "That I will bear true faith and allegiance to the same" Repeat. "That I will obey the orders of the President of the United States. That I take this obligation freely, without any mental reservation or purpose of evasion. And that I will well and faithfully discharge the duties of the office of Private in the Psy Guard of the United States upon which I am about to enter. So, help me God."

As the last words passed his lips a feeling of bondage came over him. There was no experience within Drew's life that could compare to the realization that he had just pledged his life's purpose to his country. It was not something he was ashamed of, but he felt he was left helpless. He thought he should have put it off until he had experienced more in life.

The ideas swirling through Drew's head were pointless. There was no escaping his duty now.

"Congratulations private Darby, you are doing a great service to your nation." Mr. Harkins let a glow of pride emit from his façade as he watched the young man fight with his mind over his new obligation. "I apologize for the secrecy up until now, but we required your service to the United States Army's Psychic Operations. The recruits are few and far bet…"

He was interrupted by Drew who just realized what branch of the military he had just joined. "Psychic Operations? I am not psychic! How could I…"

Another interruption. "Private!" Mr. Harkins voice boomed throughout the tiny room. "I understand you have not been through basic, but in the service, we do not interrupt our superiors. I was trying to explain to you that you show promise for being able to acquire the necessary skills to operate as a psychic operative. This may not mean seeing the future; there are many specialties that fall under that category." He looked at his associates who stood stone-like at attention. "But just like any other branch you will be required to go through basic, be assigned a specialty, and then work within that grade."

Drew largely ignored the words as they echoed around the room instead choosing to focus on the word psychic. He did not believe in psychics, which left him in a reality that made about as much sense as Saturday morning cartoons. He looked up at Mr. Harkins, looking for some kind of guidance, but all he got was a hard stare.

They stood in silence for what felt like hours and ended with the older man leaving the room.

Major Smith stepped forward and in a near robotic tone he explained the current situation to Drew. "At this point we will administer the ASPVAB, Armed Services

Psychic Vocational Aptitude Battery. Major Wallace here will be participating in the examination with you." The white man stepped forward at the mention of his name.

Major Wallace, who was appearing younger as the minutes went by, spoke to Drew in what sounded to be the same voice as Major Smith. "If you have any questions or concerns please ask them now or wait until we have concluded the exam."

Drew was too flabbergasted to cover the questions that he wanted to ask. Why him? What was he going to have to do? How could he leave his life behind even for just short bursts? But all he could get out… "If I did alright on the ASVAB, then why did they tell me to go over the answers again?"

"Just wanted to make sure you didn't make any errors, the minimum score to qualify for the Psi Guard is very strict." Major Wallace showed no emotion in his response and he turned to Major Smith the second he finished speaking.

Both men turned their backs to Drew so the voice could have come from either. "Then let's begin. Private Darby please stand in the center of the room."

He did so trying to accept the culture of the military by following directions with no objections.

"There will be ten short sections that will test your initial ability in the Psi arts. Your attention to detail and your intuition to act on the puzzle we put before you shows promise for your ability to gain perception of the hidden world. You may do well in some of the tests and poorly in others. Do not worry about your score; we will analyze your results to place you in the appropriate position." There was a pause. "We will now begin."

One of the men came up from behind Drew and wrapped his arms around him. Drew struggled from the man fearing many things from the situation. There was a stigma of sorts with male on male affection and that stigma suddenly made a lot of sense to Drew. He wanted to punch the man, he wanted to run and scream for help, but before he could truly react to the unwelcomed hug the other spoke again.

"Do not worry; we just need a close connection to you. Please tell me how Major Smith feels right now."

"What?" Drew thought he was in some perverted hidden camera show. "What do you mean how he feels, feel him yourself!" The whole situation began to feel very unreal.

"Please do not speak to me that way private! I mean what emotions is he feeling right now?"

"How would I know? This doesn…"

"Calm down private. Take a couple of deep breaths and then focus on Major Smith. Tell me what he is feeling right at this moment."

Drew, realizing he had no way out of the situation, did as he was told. He thought about Major Smith, but nothing came to him. There was no realization or sudden connection all he could think was that the Major was annoyed with Drew's reaction.

"Annoyed." As soon as the words came out of his mouth, the Major let go.

He turned to face the two military men. "Well, Am I right?" Disdain clearly oozed from his voice.

Major Smith looked at him with a tweak of his neck. "Those were my thoughts, not my emotions. I was happy. But in regards to that lets move on to telepathy."

Major Wallace briskly walked to face Drew seeming like a tidal wave of authority coming at him. The major bored a stare into Drew's eyes that unnerved him so much he thought the Major's face was morphing as they stood there. Major Wallace spoke straight into Drew's mind. They were not words as much as thoughts. Rather than hearing a sentence, it was an idea that became realized in his head. It was a threat of violence, it was the notion that Drew was trapped in the room with the two men and he was about to be physically destroyed.

It was all the incentive Drew needed. He backed up from Major Wallace slamming his back into Major Smith who grabbed him from behind in a bear hug. Drew kicked his feet and achieved a front mule kick to Major Wallace's chest pushing him back a couple of feet. He struggled to free himself and try to subdue the army man who was holding him when another thought overtook his fear. This one was one of calmness and kindness. He understood he was not in danger and was only being tested.

Major Smith let Drew go as he quit struggling and Major Wallace retorted, "You seem to be a natural at telepathy. Congratulations on that."

Drew was exhausted from his day. The frights had

been coming and going leaving him in a strange fight or flight mode similar to an energized drunkenness he had only experienced the couple of times he snuck alcohol out of his parents' cabinet. He looked back and forth between the two men waiting for direction, but after a couple of minutes he became agitated. "What do you…"

With all the force of a bull Major Smith yelled, "DO NOT SPEAK!"

Major Wallace turned his attention to Drew's eyes bearing down on his soul. The color of his eyes seemed to move from their deep blue to a more fiery color. The presence of the Major caused a strange claustrophobic feeling in Drew as ideas came to him again in the same forced manner as before. He understood his instructions; speak back to Major Wallace with his mind not his mouth.

Drew strained his brain, contorted his face, and stretched out his fingers. For no particular reason he envisioned a cow and he did everything he could to force that bovine into the mind of the Major before him, but with the lack of recognition on the man's face Drew had no idea if he was successful.

The tests went on and on trying to create things out of nothing, predict what card would be pulled out of a deck, trying to look into the dining room without leaving the room he was in… But after a couple of hours of mind games that hours earlier would have seemed like a joke, Mr. Harkins returned to the room.

"Congratulations, kid. You excel in a couple of areas

and you will have a significant career in the Psi Guard. But I am going to need to have you go out back and wait for the bus." Mr. Harkins stepped aside expecting the boy to follow his directions, but he was not used to this sixteen year-old's tendencies for pushback.

"Bus? To where? My shift is almost over, I need to go home. I have homework." He blathered on while Mr. Harkins smacked himself in the forehand, open handed hoping some sense would be smacked into the boy by osmosis.

"Calm down private. You are now enlisted in the United States Army and as such you are required to attend six weeks of basic. Now go out back and wait for the bus to take you to basic." The man felt he was dealing with a toddler, but his deep breathing and attempt at rationality was helping him keep his sanity.

"But my parents? You said I would be gone in short bursts. Who will tell them where I am? What about my school work?" Again Drew just rambled until Mr. Harkins cut him off.

"STOP TALKING!" He dropped the possibility of reasoning with Drew and went into his military personality. "Major Wallace is here to be your double. He will assume the role of Drew Darby completing all of your school, family and social obligations."

Drew chuckled showing his lack of respect and maturity, but there was no way Major Wallace could pass for him, not at school and definitely not at home. He turned back to look at the Major, but the vision was shocking. Major Wallace had lost all of his muscle mass and was starting to look somewhat like Drew. "What the Hell?" Drew backed into the wall as if he was being introduced to a ghost.

Drew's voice came out of Major Wallace's mouth full with the puberty cracks, "Sorry to frighten you, but I am what you would call a shape shifter. Doubling for a new recruit is what I do, so don't worry about a thing; I can keep your life held together nicely."

"But how do you know how I act and where I live and what my schedule is and who I know and…"

Mr. Harkins looked down at the boy happy to see the end of the conversation in sight. "Just get on the bus, kid. We are all a part of the Army's Psychic Operations. We know more than we want to."

And with that Drew accepted his fate and brushed past Mr. Harkins. He stared at the rubber tiled floors as he slowly slumped through the kitchen to the back door. In an attempt to take in the enormity of the day he clanked the bar on the exit door exposing himself to the bright afternoon sunlight.

He looked at the sides of the building contemplating making a run for it, but it would be no use, he would be caught. How could he run from the psychic military? He turned his focus to his shoes. Tears welled up in his eyes under the realization that he may have just condemned himself to years of his own personal Hell, the end of his childhood, the end of the world as he knew it. Even if he could get out of his new obligation the new understanding that the physical world was different than he knew could never change. That glass had shattered already.

Looking up Drew saw a light green bus stopped just a couple of feet in front of him. He had not noticed a sound, no vibration, no nothing, the bus just seemed to appear. It was a testament to his worry as opposed to another supernatural occurrence. The door swung open with a perfect A sharp tone and the driver looked down at Drew.

He was an old man with short mangy hair and a green tie-dyed shirt. He motioned for Drew to board the vehicle and when he obliged the driver slammed the doors shut. "Have a seat kid. You are our last recruit to grab. Next stop inter-dimensional basic."

THREE

MARCH! YOU OR ME

The bus ride was long and boring, weaving around mountains and down into a desert that none of the boys knew was there, but eventually they appeared at the camp. It was early evening when they arrived. All five of the recruits filed off the bus prepared for whatever boot camp had in store for them.

"I need all of you to remove your shoes and file into the reception hall," a man screamed at the new recruits before they all had reached solid ground. "Keep your shoes in your right hand, enter the building, stand behind an empty desk, and wait for the processing clerk." That was all the drill sergeant had to say. He turned his small chiseled body away from the boys and quickly heel-toed his way to the reception hall.

The group did as they were told and found themselves waiting for the processing clerk for hours. Drew was scared as he had heard many horror stories about basic training and refused to do anything wrong. His legs wobbled and his head swam with the pain of stillness, but he refused to give in.

Eventually, the processing clerks came and each recruit was allowed to sit down at their desk. There was a bunch of paperwork at that point. They filled out their next of kin, medical history, created new bank accounts…

After they each finished their paperwork, they were told to leave the hall and put their shoes on to wait for their drill sergeant. This was followed by a couple more hours of waiting. They stood in silence waiting for the man, well into the early night hours.

"You boys still here?" The drill sergeant screamed as he walked into view. "What we have now is PT Test number one. Do not move before I blow my whistle. Once I blow my whistle, I want all of you to drop and give me seventeen push-ups!" There was no warning, the whistle blew and the group of boys who were not exactly in shape fell to the ground and began to do push-ups.

A spindly boy to Drew's left coughed and hacked as he forced his arms to push his body up. Drew refused to pay any attention to his physical reaction to the situation. He just did his push-ups like he was told.

Drew returned to his feet as the drill sergeant looked down at the other four boys who seemed to be having difficulties. "You don't seem to understand. If you can't do what I am telling you then you will be shipped off to fat camp and trust me you don't want to go there." The drill sergeants perfectly squared off flat top made small moves to each side as he yelled at the children.

The push-ups were followed by sit-ups which garnered the same reaction from the boys, but the one mile run was what really got to the recruits. They were to run one mile in under eight and a half minutes. Drew forced himself to accomplish the feat. His lungs burned in the cool air, his legs wobbled from the weight of his small frame, but he made the mark. He was only one of two to do it though. The other was a thicker boy who did not appear to be having the breathing difficulties Drew had.

The drill sergeant was not kidding about fat camp, the rest of the recruits were shipped off immediately and Drew and his compadre were shown to their barracks.

"It is currently oh one hundred hours. I will be back for the two of you at oh four thirty!" The short man turned on his heel and left the two kids alone in the large warehouse of a hotel room.

Drew looked around the room and was left cold with the feeling of emptiness. The room housed thirty two bunk beds, sixty four individual mattresses. There was a small trunk at the end of each bunk and one toilet in a small room at the end of the building. Drew went to introduce himself, but the other boy had already chosen a bed and was pulling down the covers. "My name is Drew." It was not a normal move for Mr. Darby, but the emptiness he felt drove him to seek out some kind of companionship.

The husky boy looked over at him with true worry in his voice he let out, "I'm Sam." Sam paused from his mission of getting in bed to steady his breathing.

Drew did not like the effort it was taking to start a conversation, but he was determined to get his mind on something. "So, are you psychic?"

The boy looked up at him with relief on his face. "So we are truly at Psi Basic? I thought they were lying to me so they could lock me up for eternity. Thank goodness." Sam collapsed on his bed and let a smile shine through his chunky face. "But, no I wouldn't say I'm psychic. I am an OBE person."

Drew was realizing that there was going to be a serious learning curve in these psychic terms. "OBE?"

"Out of Body Experience. I use my soul and leave my body at night so I can travel around the world and see things. I was doing a projection when…"

"Projection?"

"That is what you call it when you leave your physical body. But anyway, where was I? Oh. I was projecting to Australia because I've never been there, when I ran into another person who was projecting. He was in full military uniform and chased me around. Apparently he followed me home. The next morning on my walk to school I was picked up by the Army and questioned about someone named Lucky."

"Who is Lucky?" Drew had lost focus on the barracks and was entrenched in the story.

"I don't know. They kept asking what intentions I was planting in Sydney and when was the last time I got an order from Lucky. It did not make a bit of sense, but eventually they gave me these weird tests and told me I was joining the Psi Ops of the US Army."

"That is why I am here too. The Psychic Operations… Or Psi Guard… Whatever that is."

"You don't know about the Psi Ops? Wow, I didn't know they let non-communes in."

"What is a non-commune?"

Sam was flabbergasted by Drew's lack of knowledge. He sat upright in his bed trying to decide if he should stay up all night explaining how the world worked to Drew or if he should get some shut eye. He took a deep breath. "In the paranormal world there are those who are in the know called the community and those who are not, the non-communes." Sam laid back in bed in attempt to get some kind of rest while he explained the world to Drew. "There are a lot of different areas of paranormal, I am into the OBEs, but there is also telekinesis, fortune telling, and dream walking… The military has a special force of these so called psychics. It was supposed to be a full sized army, but the inability to find willing soldiers who are capable of such abilities left them with a huge military base and few soldiers."

"Hence the big empty barracks."

"You got it." Sam continued telling the stories of the hidden world to Drew until four thirty in the morning when the short muscular drill sergeant busted through the door.

"You got ten minutes. Make your bunk, get dressed in the sweats in your locker, clean your area, and don't forget to shit, shave, and shower."

This left the two boys in a chaotic rush to accomplish what the sergeant demanded. Neither accomplished it, but the drill sergeant didn't seem to mind. He watched them bumble around the building until he had seen enough. "Kids! ATTEN-TION!"

Sam and Drew scampered back to their bunks where they stood straight up with half buttoned shirts and dripping hair. "Alright. Since we only have the two of you, we will finish your processing today. Basic information, issue your uniform, get your hair done, and then we will be off to basic."

Both Sam and Drew thought they were in basic already, but held their tongue as they knew speaking out would not help the situation.

"Once you are there you will buddy up and start your training - physical, educational, and mental. Let's head back to reception to finish up."

FOUR

ASK WHERE'S IT AT

Drew and Sam sat inside a contraption that was best described as a wall-less elevator. The large platform holding the two boys and their drill sergeant shook ever so slightly as they were gently drawn toward the mountains.

The boys were curious about where they were headed, but they remained silent due to the couple days of training they had received at the reception battalion. They learned of the correct name for the miniature base they had arrived at as their uniforms were issued. Now as they left their place of processing for their true basic training the two boys looked like brothers. Both with hair barely visible above the scalp, dressed in fatigues, their body shapes and Drew's glasses were about the only things making them distinctive.

The similarity in their looks was apparent to the young men, but they had taken the loss of their identity as a given, being a part of the military. The idea that they were supposed to trust each other with their lives seemed a little more plausible when they were hard to distinguish from one another.

The trip was slow and boring, but if Drew had learned anything his short time in the army, it was to not ask unnecessary questions unless he wanted some immediate exercise. They sat upon old vinyl covered plush benches as the flat platform grazed over the dirt inching closer and closer to the mountains.

The sun was high and the temperature was seasonably hot leaving the boys in some discomfort since they were entirely covered in camo, which worked as a sauna on their bodies. As the heat became more intense, Drew began to feel faint. He thought he might not stay conscious all the way to their destination. His vision began to go darker. Sparkly purple static began to invade his sight. He shook his head to regain focus risking a few push-ups in the process, but he figured a little punishment was better than his drill sergeant thinking he was not fit enough for basic and ending up in fat camp.

Drew's sight returned to normal except for a noticeable clump of the purple-y static, but the static did not follow his gaze. It stayed on a single point upon the mountain as if to point out some aspect of that area. The idea that the small indention in the mountain where the static hung in his vision was of any importance did not hit him. Instead, Drew tried to focus on staying awake through the torturous heat.

The odd vibrational sound of the floating platform forced Drew and Sam into a sort of hypnotic state. They stared off into the surrounding area in a near daydream as the platform made contact with the mountain. There was no crash or abrupt stop. Instead the platform sank into the mountain as if it were a hologram, and they descended into a dark pit, still spellbound by the humming of the machine.

Their foggy state kept them from gasping with surprise and instead just incorporated their current reality with a normalcy that they had never known. The dark tunnel they seemed to be lowering into caused the sounds to echo and reverberate against the cavernous walls that were not visible in such blackness.

The temperature dropped significantly, as they continued down, Drew began to see the purple static pop back into his vision. It formed a sort of conveyer belt in the darkness as if he could hop off the platform he was on and ride the static formed escalator back out of the hole.

The appearance of the static held Drew's attention only for a moment as the darkness subsided to a glorious view of a small military camp obviously far below the surface of the Earth. The boys slowly fell out of their stupor as they laid eyes on the small encampment.

It was a shimmer of hope in the vast darkness of the hole. There were no discernable cave walls surrounding the camp, it just looked like a little base in the midst of nothing. It was a simple makeshift town with a few barracks, a mess hall, a couple of housing units for the drill sergeants, a watch tower, and a few temporary buildings scattered about. But it wasn't the architecture that was inducing awe in the boys, it was the liveliness of the light that danced from buildings off into the depressing darkness.

A speaker in the floor of their elevator spoke at them. "Welcome to Fort Inspire. This will be your location for the next several weeks. We are a state-of-the-art training facility where you will learn all that is necessary to begin your duty as a psi ops enlistee. Everything that is required for your health and wellbeing will be afforded to you. For those who are well versed in the psychic disciplines, please be aware that there is a protection over this base. Anyone who is opposed to our mission will not be able to enter without an escort." The speaker let off a small humming buzz as it switched off.

Drew smirked at the idea that the military was still using an old fashioned speaker for their "state-of-the-art facility", but decided against calling attention to it. The platform stopped just feet away from the fort with a sudden jolt.

The boys followed their drill sergeant off the platform and into the base where they would finally receive their training.

FIVE

THE NOVEMBER OF THE

Major Wallace lay in Drew's bed staring up at the ceiling disappointed with his current mission. He had doubled for a prince, a millionaire, and a rock star. Unfortunately, Drew's life was nothing but boring and sad. There was nothing fun that Major Wallace walked into, just school, work, and family time.

There wasn't even a challenge in his new assignment. As a shape shifter he not only morphed to the body of his target, but he also could hone in on the target's thoughts and past. The inter-dimensional radiation left from past events was very apparent to his kind and assuming those thoughts and memories was quite a simple task.

Major Wallace closed his eyes trying to get some sleep before he started spending time in high school being ridiculed for his lack of social ability.

The next morning Major Wallace awoke at his normal military time, but had to wait for Drew's mother to wander into the room in an attempt to get him out of bed. It was the ritual of Drew and his mother, which Major Wallace was supposed to abide by until he could start gradually changing things so the normal world would not notice the post boot camp changes in Drew.

It was the beginning of Major Wallace's first full of day being Drew Darby, and he could not wait for it to end. At least he would get a report from Fort Inspire today informing him of Drew's progress, change in daily habits and thoughts so he could begin the transition. A couple of hours went by before Wendy, Drew's mother, came in to wake him up.

Major Wallace used Drew's squeaky young voice to whine and complain about how he did not want to get up. The act of whining grated at Major Wallace's nerves, he hated people who complained, but his career required it.

Eventually he rose, grabbed some painfully outdated clothes and wandered across the hallway to shower. It was a moment of staring in the mirror that Major Wallace realized he had a lot of work ahead of him. He stood naked staring into the reflection looking over the young body of Drew. There was an obvious mishandling of the body. When he should have been fit and lively there was nothing but a saggy depressed body. And even though Major Wallace could just alter his appearance, he was going to have to do the manual labor, the physical workouts so others would believe the change was occurring.

As he stepped into the shower he felt an incoming message hit his brain. It was an update on Drew. He understood that Drew was making large strides in physical fitness as well as mental confidence. It was time for him to begin the change of Drew's social life.

Standing there washing his body Major Wallace could envision Drew's current situation at the camp. To the Major's surprise, Drew was already down in the cave, no sunlight of any kind, but he was conversing with people. In the few days there, he seemed to have built up confidence in speaking to females as well as non-awkward social conversation. It caught Major Wallace off-guard, but brought a smile to his face.

He let the transmission fade into his memory as he finished his shower. He came out into the living room, looked Wendy in the eyes with the most innocent stare he could muster and talked to his "mom". "It's still a little early and for some reason I feel like a jog. I think I'll go out and run around the block."

Wendy was in shock from the initiative her son just displayed. He had never volunteered for exercise once in his life, but she was not about to discourage him. Instead, she smiled and nodded, watching in disbelief as her boy went out the front door to get his jog in.

The exercise was a nice return for Major Wallace, although he was not a fan of real workouts or weightlifting, the jogging made him feel healthy. He sprinted around the neighborhood slowing down for the section near his house so his mother would not see him overachieving.

Major Wallace finished his morning by walking around the house, preparing his books and eating breakfast.

The short drive to school was something that the Major had not grown accustomed to. He arrived at school ten minutes or so before the first bell. In order to begin building the perceptual confidence of Drew by his classmates, he wandered down the halls looking for someone to talk to who would not reject him.

Feeling the radiating memories of the past while reading the thoughts of his classmates in the present became a difficult task. As he swept by most of the kids he was inundated with abusive thoughts such as dork, geek, or worse. Even Major Wallace began to internalize some self-deprecation while he mentally relived some of Drew's life.

The insults and pain seemed to be never ending even as he passed by Drew's secret infatuation. The past memories were thick around Daisy. She was a tall lanky girl with badly cut brown hair and an excess of makeup. She had freckles that brought attention to her damaged glasses and blunt cut hair. She looked at the interim Drew with the same disgust as the rest of the children, but Drew's past memories of her were so thick they almost impaired Major Wallace's vision of the girl. He could not feel her memories past Drew's.

He did not understand the interest in the girl. She was plain at best, and the Major had always gravitated toward the exceptional, not to mention it was hard for him to find any type of sexual interest in a girl half his age.

He marked the girl in his mind as a project that Drew would appreciate the Major working on, but right now he had to find someone to talk to. As the trek continued, now with only six minutes before the morning bell, the Major trotted past more and more of the abusive classmates.

He began to lose hope until he came across a girl crouched in the corner by herself. She was obviously one of the oldest kids in the school, visually too old for high school, but she could have failed a few grades. She was wearing knee high black boots, a black skirt that came down to the top of the boots, and it was topped off with a black shirt of a small kitten that had a thought bubble that said "I am so cute, I am gonna kill myself".

When Major Wallace stopped his movements to speak to the girl, she didn't seem to have any preconceived notions about Drew, so she was the best candidate for a new friend. He stood over her once he had approached the corner she inhabited. Looking down he could see the blond roots peeking out from underneath her black hair donned with black lace bows.

He pushed out his new crackling voice. "Mind if I sit?"

The girl looked up at him showing her plump face painted with black lipstick, black eyeliner, black eye shadow, and a pale powder. "My world is unaffected by your location in it."

He almost laughed in the girl's face, but, trying to build some sort of rapport with anyone in Drew's school, he resisted the urge. Ignoring his own experiences from high school he searched for the right words. He could not rely on his life with his football successes, his high popularity, or his social achievements. This girl was different. He scanned her thoughts hoping to find a clue to conversation, but she was already ignoring him and flying in her own demented world of thought.

Reading her thoughts he could see her wandering through the school slashing her classmate's throats. The blood of her victims pooled up on the ground and dripped down her dark outfit as she splashed through it in her boots. Torturous pleas came from each child that she murdered in her thoughts. And she laughed at their pain. In her mind she was extending her own misery to the weak, but Major Wallace saw it as an opportunity.

He sank down against the wall next to her, too close for her to feel comfortable. "None of these people understand our plight." He planted the seed for their friendship with his ridiculous comment.

She looked over at him with an unrealistic snarl on her face, "You feel the intensity of the world's misery?"

Major Wallace again pushed back a guffaw as he felt the girl trying to speak in some glorious code. "There is nothing but hatred in this world, and I am one of the few who can feel it."

The hefty girl shoved her pudgy little hand in the Major's face. "Sarah, but call me Sin."

Major Wallace smirked as he reached out to shake the girl's hand. "Drew, but it doesn't matter." He attempted to keep his somber demeanor as he exchanged pleasantries. As he was about to make contact with the girl's hand, the bell rang.

He stood to go to class and Sin looked up at him. "You're actually going to go get indoctrinated by their conformist academics?"

"Nothing better to do."

"Sucker." That was all Sarah said as she got to her feet and wandered out the door of the school.

Major Wallace sauntered through the halls to his class making it just in time to not be tardy. He felt a small triumph in finding someone who would talk to him, but at the same time he was again being barraged by negative thoughts about Drew. He slid into his chair attempting to ignore all the thoughts. It was far from an easy task, but he managed to focus on the lesson which was far below his level of thinking.

The best thing about the Major's mission was that he did not have to use much brain power to keep Drew's A average up in school. He spent more time trying to figure out how to fix his reputation in order for Drew to keep his spirits up while he was at home. The last thing they needed was a Psi soldier depressed about life because of high school drama.

The day went on as normal. Major Wallace did his job of being Drew and kept to himself, but he did let some people begin to see the transformation of Drew into the soldier he was truly becoming. He held his head up when he walked. He let a small swagger enter his gait. Just a couple of hints to show people what would be around the corner.

On his way out of the building to his car he ran across Sarah who was writing poetry in the grass. She noticed him as he walked by. "Hello Drew but it doesn't matter."

Major Wallace gave her a quick head nod.

"How was your brainwashing today? Did you conform to their beliefs?"

The Major was not in a mood to pretend to be dark and brooding, but his job forced him. "Just the normal vomit they force into the gasmasks they call education."

She let a smile come out of her half wiped off black lips as she transcribed the boy's impromptu poem. "For once I am glad I have met someone. You understand things Drew but it doesn't matter."

Major Wallace nodded his head as if she was enlightening him to the secrets of the world.

She raised her hand toward him. "Help me up?"

The Major reached down grabbing her hand to bring her to her feet when a rush of exhaustion hit him. All of his breath and sensation rippled through his body and out of his hand. He collapsed to the grass into a puddle of Drew.

Sin scooted back from the Major in fear of the sudden crumpling of the visual Drew. As soon as she let go of his hand he could breathe again. As his breathing returned to normal and he opened his eyes, a panicked Sarah was standing over him. "Are you ok?" The darkness had left her demeanor and she was showing true compassion which she had not wanted to do.

The thoughts of the girl poured into Major Wallace's mind. Her thoughts were basic and superficial, surprising the Major. He had expected more depth in the girl. It was as if she trying to convince her own mind of her intentions.

The fake Drew got to his hands and knees letting her know that he was alright. But, as she reached under his arms to help him to his feet, he collapsed again, the world going black, his pulse rate slowing dangerously low.

Forcing his eyes closed trying to regain his breath again he thought to himself, "Of all the kids I could have befriended, I had to choose an energivore."

SIX

SOLDIERS OR ALL OF US

Major Wallace had not looked forward to Tuesday night as he was to receive no sleep. He had to schedule his briefings for some point each week when he could spend eight to ten hours communicating with the base as to how his mission was coming along even though the briefings rarely took more than an hour or two. Only a day had passed since his energy was stolen by Sin the energivore, but he had managed to convince her that he was ill and not alert her to her abilities.

Sarah, or Sin, did not appear to be aware of her power to suck the energy out of other beings. Not a surprise, since humans were one of the least vulnerable species in the world. Major Wallace, being a shape shifter, was much more susceptible to her powers. The only experience Major Wallace could imagine that she could have noticed would most likely be construed as cats and dogs just enjoying a nap in her lap.

He was able to communicate with her easily without touching her and again having the energy sapped out of him, but her existence complicated his mission and would be a major aspect of his briefing that night.

He laid on his bed and watched the clock change to nine p.m. There was nothing left but to keep his nodes of communication open for the messages from the base. He lay back in the youthful bed atop the red and black bedspread that constantly reminded Major Wallace he was subbing in for a child. The air felt crisp as the temperature had turned cool inside the house bringing Major Wallace to a good state of relaxation when words began to fill his head.

'Please report, Major. What is the status of your target's transition?' The familiar yet official words clamored around in his brain.

Major Wallace focused his thoughts in preparation for the telepathy for which, after just a few days, he was sorely out of practice. He tried to express himself in full sentences, but he was only able to extend general thoughts.

The base received and recorded the odd broken thoughts as 'physical transition began, social transition began, behavioral transition began.'

The clerk who was transcribing the report sent out another transmission. 'There seems to be interference with your transmission. I am in front of a keyboard and am going to switch over to automatic writing. I will send a personality packet to you so you can write the report yourself.'

The switch was common for a new Psi Guard clerk. The switch to automatic writing only meant that the clerk was too lazy to transcribe and preferred to give control of his body over to the soldier who was reporting. It annoyed Major Wallace turning his night from a meditative telepathy to a more exhaustive night of body possession, but his telepathy skills were too weak to argue.

He sat up in the boy's bed and focused on relaxing his body. He forced his toes numb, then his feet, his legs… Before long Major Wallace sat in the bed eyes closed with a vision of just his floating head unattached to anybody. He let his spirit drift away into the space of the bedroom. Opening his spiritual eyes he could see himself propped up on the bed, back leaned against the wall. Seeing one's self was an odd experience the first few times, but for someone like Major Wallace this was just a confirmation that he could still leave his body.

The travel to the base was instantaneous and not something that was visually describable. Instead it was more of existing inside a tunnel of the sense of touch, a vortex of sensation that stimulated his non-existent body from the outside.

Once he reached the base he immediately found the clerk whose personality had conveniently been transmitted to his brain. The boy was young and youthful, but suffered from one of the most common ailments of soldiers, buyer's remorse. After realizing what he had gotten himself into with his eight year commitment to his country, he wanted out, but it was not an option. Instead he would spend his nights forking over his body to strange military men so they could type up reports without having to waste taxpayer's dollars on extra computers or long distance communication. He was there because he was cheaper than technology. The human brain was capable of these great feats as long as there was a willing body on the other end.

Major Wallace drifted down from the rafters of the small army building and soaked his spirit into the body of the young clerk. The tenseness in the boy's shoulders, the aroma of his new self, and the excessive amounts of energy running through his hands gave him more input on what it would be like to be a kid like Drew instead of just impersonating him. It made him realize how much more he was like a teenager when he was at the school as opposed to being at home.

He opened the eyes of the clerk and reached out for the keyboard. Knowing that there were generals waiting to read the report in real time on their PCs, Major Wallace immediately began typing.

Physical Transition

Status:

The physical transition has begun. On an hourly basis I am making visual modifications to my appearance, so that upon the return of Private Darby to his body, his new physique, that basic has given him, will not alert the civilians in his life. The visual changes amount to less than a millimeter change per hour in the perceived fat and muscle on the body.

Requirements:

In order to portray the correct visual of Private Darby I will require daily updates on the visual transformation of his body along with a projected finished product.

Behavioral Transition
Status:
The behavioral transition has begun. On a daily basis I have transitioned the family to become accustomed to both physical activities such as running and working out as well as changes in respect and manners. I have also been acquainting his classmates to a slightly adjusted attitude with an attempt at new friendships and courtesy toward others.
Requirements:
None

Social Transition
Status:
The social transition has begun. A new friendship has been created during the time the Private has spent away from home. It is with a young girl by the name of Sarah who prefers the alias Sin. She is considered a gothic by modern standards with a draw toward the negative.
Requirements:
In order for Private Darby to assimilate back into his life he will need to be briefed multiple times about the new connections his body has made with complete synopsis of who they are and what he knows about them.

Notes:
There is an issue with Private Darby's new friendship. The

girl who goes by Sin is an unaware energivore. She has sapped my energy…

Major Wallace felt an enormous tug from the back of his head. He went limp as his soul ejected from the young clerk's body. Someone had yanked on his silver cord, a tether of sorts that connects the soul to its original body, and now he was traveling through space back to his shape-shifted body.

It was less than a couple of seconds when he found himself sitting on Drew's bed just as he had been before he possessed the clerk to write his report. The only difference was that he was staring at the Psy Ops force General who had evidently just teleported to the location. The man was huge, an easy seven feet tall and over four hundred pounds. General Pounder was what the man demanded to be called; of course, it was unknown if that was his real name or one that he created as an alias to his civilian identity.

He stood there in his well decorated uniform dwarfing anything that happened to be near him. His squared-off jaw tensed from side to side as he waited for Major Wallace to regain his composure before he began yelling. Once Major Wallace realized what was in store, he opened his mouth to remind the General that there were unsecured civilians within the home who would be within earshot of the tirade. He did not speak once he noticed the staleness of the air and lack of traffic noise from outside the window. It clued him in to the fact that General Pounder had stopped time. He closed his mouth waiting for the tirade.

"You come across a restricted being that attacked you, government property, and you wait to inform us by a briefing?" The General was fuming with anger. His face was getting pinker by the second and to the Major's astonishment, he seemed to be growing in size as well.

"General Pounder, sir. I was never in any danger because the girl is unaware of her abilities."

"I do not care what she is aware of. She has attacked a soldier in the United States Army. Because of that she should be apprehended, and it should be made sure that she has no knowledge of Lucky or his army." There was a pause as Pounder contemplated the situation. "I should have you thrown in the brig for this."

"Sir, she is of no danger and I mean no disrespect, but there is no need to bring her in just to find out she knows nothing. I can handle her; she is still in high school for Christ's sake." The Major spoke of her school status as opposed to her age as he vividly recalled her looking older than the others. He cringed at the return fire he would receive from the comment, but when he is being threatened with incarceration he had to present a rebuttal.

"So be it. You will not be held accountable given that you obtain all necessary information from this Sin before you put another soldier in danger when Private Darby returns to his life." General Pounder was calming with an obvious decrease in blood circulation as he crept back toward his normal skin tone. He took a deep breath and whispered to

Major Wallace, "Major, don't let that girl find out what she is capable of."

There were no goodbyes or salutes, the world just faded away as the General dissipated into the air. The ambiance went back to its normal feel and the street outside began to rumble with traffic. Major Wallace was left with no comfort, just an additional mission.

Interrogate Sin. 'Shouldn't be too hard a quest' thought Major Wallace. 'I just need to make sure she doesn't physically touch me.' He had no idea how hard that might be.

SEVEN

IS IT TO INSPIRE OR IS IT THE CAPITAL

Drew and Sam felt lost inside boot camp. It was more than a feeling of being in over their heads. It was more of a sense that they were not on the right planet. The lack of sunlight caused confusion about the time of day. The sheer volume of drill sergeants, who all looked identical, left them constantly anxious. And even the other soldiers who were attending the basic training seemed to be more comfortable than the two boys.

The barracks at the camp were not filled. There were thirty-two bunks in each barrack, but the lack of soldiers left each of the ten buildings with two to four soldiers in each. The boys had seen the other soldiers come into the cave, but hadn't held real conversations with any of them. They appeared to be transfers from other army divisions so they were not required to process, but they did not understand why those soldiers had to redo basic training.

The biggest surprise to Drew was that the camp was co-ed. Out of the couple of dozen soldiers there were at least six females which gave Drew a small amount of anxiety as he was not exactly fluent in girl talk. Sam, on the other hand, was as relieved to see the opposite sex as was the average male teen, and he was feeling withdrawal from his interactions with them.

Nearly the entire first day inside the camp was a different experience than above ground. It was not a ton of push-ups while higher ranked men yelled at them. Instead, there was an odd situation where the drill sergeants encouraged the boys to make decisions.

They were not told when or what to eat, but instead, when they sauntered into the mess hall, they were asked what they wanted. Drew looked across the few trays of food along the counter eventually pointing to the brown meat-ish item.

A drill sergeant was looking over his shoulder explaining why his choice of chicken was a good one. He spoke of nutrients and proteins while at the same time telling Drew that he needed to speak up and be more confident...

The whole day was like this. In the evening back at Drew and Sam's lonely barrack they discussed the oddity that was their current situation.

"I've always been afraid of boot camp, but this isn't anything to worry about. I don't understand the horror stories I always heard with the screaming and exercises and danger and gas chambers and immunizations and swimming and…" Drew trailed off until Sam finally put an end to it.

"This isn't normal boot camp." Sam began, not believing Drew's inability to understand what was happening.

"We are too valuable for the military to break and convince us we aren't as important. They want us to protect ourselves. They want us to be confident leaders not subordinate grunts." Sam could not imagine what kind of intuition Drew had if he couldn't connect simple dots like the ones in front of him.

Drew laid back on his bunk letting Sam's theory sink in. The idea did not sit well with him. It felt off. He figured that the army would want them to be subordinate, they were not leaders they were just considered a rarity. He thought there was a better chance that some kind of mind control was used in normal basic that these soldiers may be too aware of. The whole idea was just idle chatter as far as Drew was concerned and Sam's snores soon told Drew that he was not the only one who felt that way.

As Sam created some odd white noise, Drew began to daydream as he worked toward slumber. He envisioned the people he had seen around the camp that day. There were the dozen drill sergeants he had seen who all looked the same to him. There were the boys who all seemed to be at least a handful of years older than him. They all carried themselves with respect and dignity, something he felt he lacked.

Of course, being a young boy Drew's light fantasy was focused on the girls of the camp. There were only a few, but he could not help but picture their faces, their hair, and the forms of their bodies. He felt ashamed for that kind of fantasy. He was a part of something more serious, something dignified. He thought he should not defile the greatness of the military with his dirty high school thoughts. He probably gave more respect to the idea that he was military than nearly any boy before him.

But no matter how much he tried, his fantasies wandered back to the girls. The one that caught his attention most was the only blond on the base. Her hair was short and boyish as were the styles of all the female soldiers. She reminded him of Daisy back at school. She had the same lanky figure and somewhat awkward features that his crush back at home had. Truthfully, his fantasies of holding this mysterious blond girl and running his fingers through her hair weren't actually fantasies about her, they were fantasies of Daisy with a different face, different body.

It was another one of those inconsistencies within his own mind that he just had not noticed. As Drew slipped out of fantasy and into slumber Sam's snores morphed into words and the boy spoke in his sleep. It was a soft voice and much deeper than Sam's waking tone. "The darkness. Walk toward it. The Psi will show you the way." The words sank into the background in a way that kept Drew's conscience from recognizing them. It was just a whisper to his sleeping mind leaving a small suggestion within him.

As Drew fell into sleep his dream body wandered the base. A low rumble guided him toward the center of camp. The rumble was actually the words coming from Sam, but they were unintelligible to dream Drew.

"Luck does not follow soldiers it kills them. The best life is discharge." The words sang from Sam's lips and spoke to Drew's subconscious while his dream just felt a vibration.

As he wandered the fort, the soothing tones of Sam's voice pulled Drew to the center of the cave-covered encampment. In his dream, just as it was in real life, the center of the camp housed another typical building. But in his dream this building was guarded by a large ghostly dog with two smaller dogs living within him. One of the smaller dogs was regal, almost as if he was higher ranked than Drew. He wanted to salute the dog. The second internal dog was frozen with icicles dripping from its fur. It shivered within the larger invisible hound. The big canine looked down upon Drew and spoke in perfect English, "It is us." There was a long pause before the dog spoke again. "We keep you inside once you decide to enter."

The dream faded as a drill sergeant entered the barrack to wake up the new soldiers. The dogs faded into a baby, a boy, and a man.

"UP! Get dressed, make your bed, shave, shit, shower! You boys got ten minutes! No excuses, no exceptions!" The drill sergeant had eliminated the dream from Drew's mind as the young boy hopped from his bed with the sudden realization that the cavernous basic training may not be as different from the normal boot camp as he thought.

EIGHT

IT MATTERS WHAT YOU DREAM OF

Drew and Sam were now able to complete the drill sergeant's orders each morning with little effort. They were standing at attention, fully dressed, and showered with ten seconds to spare. Drew forced his eyes forward forgetting his odd dream of just minutes ago.

"Kids! You will follow me to mess to get your breakfast, and then we will be going to physical training where you will be getting your schedule that you will follow for the remainder of your training. Do you understand?" The drill sergeant's voice sounded like every military movie in existence.

The boys' reaction was also identical to every military movie. "Yes Drill Sergeant!"

With that they walked out of the barrack and into the darkened camp. As they marched through the base they passed other soldiers in training all headed toward the mess hall. The darkness of the cave left no signs of the time of day. Only the clock on the face of the mess hall shed some light.

It was 04:30, but the lack of sun left the boys turned around in their ability to judge time even after just a single day at the camp.

The mess hall contained all the soldiers that were at the camp. It was not the typical sight you would see during basic training with the lack of recruits, but Sam and Drew had no experience to draw on and felt more bewildered than the others in the room. They were directed to the line that would get them fed, and they followed the directions without question proving that their teenage rebellions had already been quelled by the drill sergeants.

As had been the case the day before, Drew was asked what he wanted. He told them he would have the grey lumpy sauce stuff and the soldier dishing out the slop congratulated Drew on a good choice of grits. As he walked down the line he was handed a glass of water, a biscuit that was a little overly firm, and a plate with what he assumed were scrambled eggs on it.

Drew and Sam sat at the next open seats as the soldiers seemed to be filing into place rather than sitting in social circles. As Drew crunched into his biscuit reaching the slightly uncooked center Sam spoke up, "Maybe we get to find out how this all works today."

Drew dropped his jaw, hanging over his plate letting the food fall out of his mouth. "What do you mean?"

"We get a schedule. Maybe we will feel like we know what **is** happening once we have this schedule." Sam was wide eyed thinking about the possibility.

Drew spooned up some grits and let the applesauce consistent mixture dribble down his throat. "Maybe." He was just appeasing Sam at this point. "Isn't this stuff awful?" Drew was holding back a purge of his food.

Sam shook his hands to wave off Drew's question. "Think about it. We should know what they are going to show us here. Maybe we will know why it isn't just normal basic or why we are underground or why…"

Sam was interrupted by Drew's spittle as he spit out his first attempt at the eggs. "I think this is my last breakfast for a while."

Sam wiped off his face and continued his fantasy. "We could know what grades we could get or what weapons we get to use."

Drew was about to respond when one of the drill sergeants stood in the doorway shouting. "Breakfast is over! Throw out your trays and come with me! I will not wait for stragglers and you don't want to be caught not in class!" The large camouflaged man turned to march out of the room as all the soldiers scrambled to toss their trays in the sinks and get in formation.

Sam whimpered as he threw out his entire tray of food. "I didn't even get to take a bite."

Drew jogged past him, "You didn't miss much."

From there they went straight into physical training. Jumping jacks, squats, lunges, sit-ups. It had only been a couple of days, but the muscle burn had already dwindled down and the routines just felt like a forced boredom as opposed to a torturous punishment.

After their mile run they were handed a sheet of paper containing their schedule. It was blocked off into four groups: mess, PT, weapons training, and sleep. The basics of the schedule were wake up, eat, PT, weapons training, eat, PT, weapons training, PT, eat, sleep. The only thing that differed was the weapons training. It listed the weeks.

Weeks 1 and 2: Telepathy, Psi Generation, Remote Viewing, and OBE

Weeks 3 and 4: Psi Expulsion, Telekinesis, Thought Planting, and Possession

Weeks 5 and 6: Empathy, Seer, Dead Talking, and Dimension Hopping

The sight of so many supernatural-looking classes took the breath out of Drew. How could he possibly be involved in telepathy, telekinesis, or speaking to the dead, much less possession and dimensional travel? It was a shock about as expected as a punch to the gut. Of course, he barely had to time to think as they were marching toward their first weapons training class.

The entire population of soldiers in training filed into a small steel building with ten rows of desks lined up facing an old green chalk board at the front of the room. They all filed to the desks and sat at attention waiting for instruction.

A drill sergeant, unidentifiable from the others, stood at the front of the class, letting his booming voice echo throughout the open room. "Kids! Welcome to the basics of telepathy. Just to save me from forcing pushups on you I will just explain a few things first." There was a pause as if he was waiting for a response, but even Sam and Drew had learned too much about the military life to fall into his trap.

After a short wait and a subtle chuckle the man continued. "This is weapons training, but unlike the regular enlistees you will not have the aid of a firearm unless you were previously trained in it. The enemies we face are only slightly distracted by firearms and we utilize them only when we have no other option. Your weapons are your minds. As you should know by now, you show the potential to use functions within your brain that most men only dream of. You are the elite."

He turned his back to his audience and walked toward the board. He wrote the word telepathy on it in big block letters. "What is telepathy? It is the ability to see what another person is thinking."

Drew's mind began to wander as the drill sergeant entered into professor mode. He looked around the room recognizing most of the soldier from around the camp. He looked at Sam, sitting to his right, locked on, in his attention to the instructor. Drew peered over to his left and noticed the short blond haired girl.

He let a smile wisp across his lips as he reverted to his adolescent fantasy about the female. He thought about her body, her lips, and her breath against his neck. He could not shake his trance as he envisioned the girl in inappropriate ways.

It was the solid connection of the girl's fist with

Drew's jaw that pulled him out of his fantasy. He turned toward the girl, now standing at his desk, as his eyes welled up from the impact.

She looked down at him with vengeful eyes, "Keep me out of your thoughts you sicko,"

She was interrupted by the drill sergeant at the front of the room, "That!" He shouted louder than normal to make sure he drowned out the girl. "That is why you must learn to control your thoughts and pay attention in class." The instructor looked down at the battered Drew, "This soldier decided to pervert this class room with a sexual fantasy about his fellow soldier. And, she, reading his thoughts, did not appreciate it." He walked over to Drew creating a sickening feeling in the boy's stomach. "Imagine you are in a life threatening fight with a demon." The mention of the word demon alerted Drew to a basic fear he was unaware he had. "You can't let a demon know your fears or desires. You can't even let a demon know your next move, so if you can't even pay attention in class how are you going to protect the constitution of the United States?"

He left Drew staring at him in astonishment as he turned to return to the front of the classroom. Drew did everything in his power to focus for the rest of the class.

"Any of you who know how to use telepathy at this point got a fun scene from Private Darby over there. But this is exactly why we need to keep this power with the responsible and honest men and women of the Psi-Ops. Just imagine the intrusion of privacy and infringements of people's rights if common criminals had this power. So, I don't want to see any of you taking advantage of the abilities you develop here. You took an oath and it is treason to break it."

He stood at the front of the class letting the threat sink in. Once everyone seemed to relax a bit he returned to weapons training. "I want everybody to close their eyes and envision a tunnel connecting your brain to mine."

NINE

MAN OWNS NOTHING BUT HIS OWN SIN

Once telepathy class was over Drew wanted to run from the building to hide his embarrassment of his thoughts. But as a soldier his feelings were not necessarily his property. He had given up the ability to make his own decisions when he took that oath.

The drill sergeant from the telepathy class led the entire group out of the building and around the darkened base. They marched about with many of the recruits yawning from their skewed sense of time. The darkness of the underground camp caused lethargy much worse than jet lag. It was nearly 09:00 but it felt more like the middle of the night. Drew couldn't help but wonder if the darkness would affect his ability to deal with time when he got out of basic training.

They made a few circles around camp before Drew realized that they were just getting some exercise, but the third go round caught Drew's attention. They passed by the center of the camp, and in doing so they passed the building from Drew's dream.

Seeing the building in real life gave a chill to Drew's bones. He instinctively bowed his head to the door in a gesture that not only gave respect to the creature he envisioned in his dream, but also allowed him to pass by without having to lay his eyes on the terrifying building. He shivered from the cold that had overtaken him.

As he came within feet of the door he heard voices streaming into his mind, "It is us. Once you enter." It was a familiar voice from his dream. A second voice, a low rumble that Drew also recognized, seemed to emanate from his own mind. "Inside is the life of your dreams. Discharge is the entrance to the kingdom." The voice was barely words, almost just a vibration. As they marched away from the building the voices faded. Drew had learned his lesson from telepathy class - keep your mind focused. He let his eyes dart to his fellow soldiers, but no one else seemed the slightest bit dazed. He stared forward and kept his mind in line while they approached their next class.

Drew was not surprised that the next class was held in another ambiguous steel building, but upon entrance to the class he noticed a major difference. The drill sergeant at the front of the class was not the undistinguishable man in camo. Instead there stood a slim older looking man in a dress uniform. He carried a simple smile on his face that made the grey mass of hair almost twinkle under the florescent lighting.

The soldiers filed in as they had in telepathy class, but the drill sergeant screamed at them as they did. "Get the Hell up! Who said you could sit? Everyone down and give me twenty."

The room filled with a silent moan that any other group of soldiers may not have noticed. The slapping of hands against concrete pattered like a new rainstorm of soldiers falling to the ground. Before they could finish the drill sergeant was shouting again. "This is a point that each of you need to remember. This is still boot camp. This is still a class of instruction. You are still learning to use your weapon with deadly force. Remember those things as we learn over the next two weeks because it is going to be fun and without those words you will think you are on vacation."

Everyone finished their pushups and stood next to their desks waiting for instruction. He asked them to sit and the group fell into their chairs in near perfect synchronicity.

The drill sergeant looked out over the classroom surveying his new students, catching glimpses of their lives through telepathy, empathy, and a couple other tricks he knew. "Everyone please close your eyes and picture a cauldron boiling in your stomach." He paced around the room watching the soldiers.

Drew closed his eyes, but his mind was wandering too much to follow the directions. He kept seeing Daisy and the blond haired girl. He was having visions of lust and greed as he imagined the three of them running wild through a mall, shopping, playing, and eating.

The drill sergeant slammed his hand down on Drew's desk stunning him out of his dreamy vision, but not before a strange occurrence happened. Just as the sound of the sergeant's smack came into Drew's ears, the faces of Daisy and the blond haired girl shifted. They lost all their features and for a split second became someone else. A tanned blond girl with a little bit of mass to her and a tall skinny dark haired girl with mangled teeth and eyes that held more emotion than any memory Drew had.

Drew dismissed the personality shift in his fantasy as he opened his eyes and focused on the old man staring him in the face. He spoke quietly with compassion as his breath bounced off Drew's face. "You are having," The drill sergeant paused as he searched for the words, "interference. Again, close your eyes."

Drew did as he was told.

"Now picture a clear box over your head. You can see out of this box and people can see you, but animals and other creatures can't. Picture a bunch of strange looking animals looking for you, but not finding you. All kinds of creatures, deer, rabbits, aliens, bugs, demons, monsters… Everything, but people."

Drew had the image in his head and before he could question the absurdity of it the drill sergeant screamed, "Ten hours!" Drew jumped, but the man was walking away before he knew what was happening.

"Now as I said, imagine a pot boiling in your stomach."

Drew closed his eyes again and to his amazement he could picture it. There were no images of girls or voices or shopping sprees, just a cauldron boiling over in his stomach.

"I want everyone to picture the liquid boiling out of the pot as a purple flashy substance so shiny it almost tingles your sight. Once you have that image, I need you to feel the pot in your stomach." He looked around to make sure the entire class was focusing. "Now feel the liquid boil up out of your stomach and into your arms and legs. It isn't hot, it doesn't hurt, but you feel it filling you up."

Drew felt the substance circulating through his body as if he was a channel and water was flowing through him. It felt almost as if it was coming both from him as well as from the earth or the sun or maybe even the moon.

"Open your eyes!" The class did as they were told. "Now, many of you will not be able to see this, but it is called psi." As the final word came from his throat a purple shiny static poured out of the man's hand.

Drew recognized it immediately as the same substance that he had seen as he entered the darkness of the mountain the day before. Only this time the static did not form a conveyer belt leading him out of the mountain, it flowed like water.

The static began to pick up its intensity flowing from both hands as well as the drill sergeants boots, ears, and eyes. Unintended gasps let the instructor know who could see it and who couldn't. He continued, "Psi is a substance that some would call energy, but that is not correct. It is actually intention and prediction. Everyone drops psi whether they mean to or not and for those who can see it naturally, it is a clue as to what people mean to do. Just as you learned earlier that you can read people's thoughts, you can also see their intent or their future. There is a difference between intent psi and predictive psi, but that is far beyond what we will be talking about. If you can see it, pay close attention to it. But beware, there are those who can control psi and they can put their own intentions into it just to divert you. But that you will be learning in Psi Expulsion, this is Psi Generation. Let's return to generating psi."

Drew sat in amazement as the drill sergeant created a tentacle of psi that emitted from his face and hung over the classroom. As his speech ended it fizzled into the background dropping bits of the static on the drill sergeant himself and the blond haired girl with such a shine it almost hurt his eyes. As the man continued his lesson Drew couldn't help but think about intentions and what it meant for the psi to land both on the instructor and the girl. Maybe Drew wasn't the only one with amorous thoughts about that girl.

TEN

IT WAS A WAY IN

The rest of Drew's day was a blur of exercise and classes. There were two more meals of randomly colored slop that Drew was praised for choosing which Sam took advantage of this time to eat. He went through two more classes of basic lessons with remote viewing and Out of Body Experiences.

He understood remote viewing to be seeing visions of current situations from a remote location. It seemed to be straight forward enough with imagining a tunnel to his target, but it did not work for him. All he saw were the three dogs from his dream. The Out of Body Experience class (or OBE) was a different beast entirely.

There were a lot of instructions regarding strange ideas that Drew did not think were possible. He was told to relax his body until his consciousness separated from his physical being, and then force his soul out of his body through his third eye, which was a symbolic eye in his forehead. Although he intended to give it a try that night as he was assigned, he couldn't find the confidence in himself that would suggest success. The rest of class was filled with symbology. They tried to explain common symbols seen in the different planes of existence and what they meant. But the lecture was pointless as Drew lacked the experience or ability to grasp the concept of separate planes of existence.

Drew was ecstatic when the day was over as he lay in his bunk trying to figure out how to eject his soul from his mind's eye.

Sam interrupted Drew's feeble attempts at OBE, "Did you enjoy the day?"

"I guess, but I am exhausted. Too exhausted to be happy I think." Drew could barely get the words out audibly as his body was starting to give out.

"I get that. But today really seemed like the beginning of…" Sam was cut off by a shocking turn of events. In the center of the barrack Drew appeared out of nowhere.

The Drew who was lying on his bunk leapt to the ground as if he was ready for battle against his new self that had just formed before his eyes. Sam had a similar reaction, but was more ready to flee than fight.

The new Drew let a smile erupt across his façade. "Drew, good to see you." He noticed the boy looking quite on edge. "Oh, sorry for the reflection there." The features of the new Drew faded away to reveal Major Wallace, the Major Wallace Drew remembered from the HappyLand back office. "I came here for some guidance, Private."

Drew tried to force down his fears and adrenaline as

he listened to Major Wallace.

"I know you don't have a lot of friends and I am working on remedying that, but I need to know what your real desires are." Major Wallace stood at attention while speaking leaving no room for any disrespect on his part.

Drew had a severe case of embarrassment torching his ears. Major Wallace had just brought up his biggest insecurity and addressed it in as flippant a way as he would someone's note taking habits. But, trying to embrace his new military mentality, Drew attempted an answer. "Well, if I am being completely honest. There is a girl named Daisy."

Major Wallace interjected before Drew was able to really humiliate himself. "That is not the type of desire I speak of. Private Darby, my job is to ensure a smooth transition for you from basic training to home. Everyone at home will be expecting you to act and look as you will upon your return. My concern is for your mental stability. You could come home and still be the invisible kid that no one pays attention to or you could be more popular. Have more friends. Not be completely hidden anymore. I really want to know, are you happy as who you are or would you like a new high school identity." Major Wallace looked back at Drew, conveniently leaving out the hurtful thoughts he heard from the other high school kids, his inability to get Daisy to speak to him, or the fact that the only friend he had made for Drew was a bigger outcast than he could imagine.

"Yes then. I would prefer to be popular." He forced the words out refusing to acknowledge the sucker punch

Major Wallace's statement dealt him.

Major Wallace nodded having already known Drew's real desires. He had only come to Fort Inspire to refocus his image of Drew. He wanted to be sure he was keeping Drew's past separated from the large amount of hateful memories other people had of the boy. "Good to know. I will try to set something up then." And with that last word the man was gone.

The two boys lay back down on their bunks and refused to speak. They let the oddity that was the end of the day float past them as they each attempted to rest.

Sam was asleep within minutes, but Drew could not get to sleep, nor could he focus enough to try his OBE homework. After nearly an hour of lying motionless in his bed he got up and wandered out the door of his barrack.

The camp was the same as it always was, dark. The lack of sky left every second of the training facility feeling like deep night. Although the clock in the center of camp seemed to keep time, Drew was doubtful that they were being told the truth about the passage of it. He wasn't sure if they were working shorter or longer days, but they didn't feel like 24 hours.

He walked out into the camp without a direction in mind, just stepping wherever his body led him. He instinctually followed the marching lines they had taken earlier in the day, but there was no one to march with, no one to watch him, just himself.

He walked for a good half hour before he stopped in

front of a building. It wasn't the building itself, but the odd feeling he got from it that keyed him into the fact that it was the building in the center of the fort, the one guarded by his three dreams dogs.

Drew instinctively saluted the invisible creature which left him with a chill and the word "us" whispered through the air as if still echoing from his dream. As the word drifted away from his consciousness a voice came into his head.

"You keep coming back here. Do you want to pass through the gates?" The strange voice came from nowhere.

"What gates? Who are you?" Drew spoke in a soft tone aware that he was not granted permission to wander the camp at night.

"I guard the gates of Hell. I am the Hell hound, the one who keeps those in Hades who enter. I am Cerberus."

Drew immediately realized the voice was the three headed dog.

There was no faint fear anymore. Drew was sprinting back to his barrack. Each step he took pounded the ground and left his mind blazing with questions. He knew what Cerberus was from his lessons on mythology from English class.

As Drew reached his barrack and closed the door behind him, he began to wonder what side he was training with - good or evil. It was questionable now that he knew the gates of Hell were on the base.

ELEVEN

TRY AND TRY AND YOU MAY GET AN A

Major Wallace had fallen into the high school routine. He got up each morning, took a shower, ran around the block, and made chitchat with Drew's parents. The small talk was by far the hardest to accomplish because he could not just talk, he had to make sure his conversations were still along the lines of a high schooler's. Otherwise, he would not be setting up Drew for an easy transition home.

The morning after his teleport to base for his quick chat with Drew was as mundane as all the others. However, he was at a loss for how to get Drew to become more popular. He kept thinking along the lines of drastic changes. He thought he could stage a riot, or a boycott on the gross lunches, or get arrested for protesting for student's rights, but they were all too grandiose. Major Wallace had spent too much time as a soldier for the United States Army Psychic Operations and all of his planning revolved around large operations.

When he arrived at school, Major Wallace

immediately went looking for Sin. He checked all the darkened corners as if he was looking for a poisonous spider, but she was not around. He searched the parking lot, the cafeteria, wasted time by the bathrooms… All in a failed attempt to speak with the energivore he had befriended, knowing that his continued employment within the military might ride on his ability to ensure the girl was not dangerous.

He spent so much time looking for her that he was late for math. He slowly walked through the halls after the late bell had rung thinking a little rebellious tardiness couldn't hurt Drew's reputation. He turned the corners of the school listening to the thoughts of the children in their classrooms. Occasionally he would hear thoughts of someone concentrating on the lesson, but largely the air was full of teenage torment. The typical heartbreak and misunderstandings of the selfish children nearly overtook the Major's concentration.

But as he neared the classroom he was to attend. He caught some thoughts about Drew. It was a memory that left someone hurt and now carrying a long ago emotional scar.

Major Wallace peered into the small window by the door to see who was in the room. Among the sea of indistinguishable children was Daisy. Her awkward lanky body was hard to focus on through the memories Drew had about the girl. He could feel all of Drew's adulation for the skinny brunette. The boy's feelings created a type of radiation that would follow her, although, completely outside of her own perceptions.

As he tried to look beyond the muddling thoughts of Drew's past, Major Wallace could almost see the memory Daisy had of Drew. It was a simple scar on her right hand that reeked of Drew's interference. He could picture the two as children younger than they are now on a playground surrounded by faceless kids.

The scene unfolded as any normal day at a park, but there was a mishap. Drew had inadvertently shoved the young Daisy, forcing her down on a rock in the ground, her blood seeping out of the small fragile hand and soaking into the girl's psyche. It was the stain that kept her from having a single positive thought about Drew. If it was not for the scar which was noticeable at all times, she might not have ever formed any opinions of the boy. It was unfortunate for him that it was still there, her permanent reminder of his vile actions.

Wallace shook his head trying to break the spell of the intoxicating vision and continued his trek to his class. Just a few feet away, he opened the door and sauntered into the class as if he was on time and acting responsibly.

The detention he got for being late to class did not bother Major Wallace, he thought it might even give him time to relax after school before he attempted the war zone that was the parking lot.

Class after class the fake Drew wandered around Drew's recollections, trying to find the same memory Daisy had. He continuously read Drew's innermost thoughts from halfway across the country, but he could not find it. Drew had forgotten about the event that scarred their relationship. He tucked the images into the back of his mind filed away to be given to Drew when he returned.

At lunchtime, Major Wallace began to look for Sin again, but it was to no avail. After deciding that she was skipping school again he ventured into the cafeteria to try to build another relationship.

He passed by Daisy preparing to apologize for the long forgotten shove, but her thoughts of disgust for Drew were too overwhelming for him to speak. It was a constant torrent of negative emotions as she stared him down repelling him like opposed sides of a magnet. He left her sight, going from table to table looking for someone who was a blank slate for Drew, but they all seemed to have predisposed ideas of the boy. Having lived in one place for the majority of his life did not help Drew.

Wallace eventually gave in and bought lunch. Picking up his tray, he realized that the cafeteria workers did not seem to have bad thoughts toward Drew, but that was not the solution for the boy's popularity issues.

The day flew by with Major Wallace feeling like a failure. He had not accomplished anything that helped him move toward his goals. He had not acquired any more information from Sin nor did he change anyone's opinion of Drew.

Class after class came and went leaving Major Wallace sitting in the room where his mathematics course was held, in detention. He just sat at his desk trying to be Drew, moping and quiet.

The teacher sat at her desk looking at the boy with a concerned look. "What is going on Drew?"

Major Wallace looked deep into his desk annoyed at the teacher's sudden urge to be a good person. He could feel her brain trying to convince itself that he was a good kid and she could save him.

"Drew, I think you may be falling in with a bad crowd." She paused as the perceived Drew refused to respond. "You haven't been stopping by to help out in the band hall. And I saw you with that woman."

Major Wallace saw Sin in the teacher's mind as she spoke. Her choice of words alerted him. "Woman?"

"The one in all black. I don't mean to judge, but people like that are not typically good influences. And, now you are in here for detention which has never happened."

"Why did you call Sarah a woman? She is my age."

"Oh." The teacher was surprised. "I've never seen her in school. And, sure you may be right, but I didn't think she was a student here."

Major Wallace pushed his annoyance down below the surface realizing that he was doing a terrible job convincing people he was Drew. "Sorry, I just have had a strange week. I guess I've been slacking in my hall monitoring duties. I'll try harder."

A smile emerged from the teacher's face boiling the anger of Major Wallace. He stood up knowing that his time was up in detention. He forced a smile as his mind cursed the woman for giving up on so many children and taking an interest in him. He thought she was pathetic, but he failed to see his own hypocrisy. He missed his own prejudice toward the kids at the school, the recruits he posed as, the people he fought in war. These thoughts never stood a chance of crossing his mind as he had already moved on to the parking lot.

He began to think like Drew, like a kid as he maneuvered out of school and out to find his car. Spotting his old hatchback among the now emptying parking lot, it locked into his mind like a target. He walked with a purpose, with a plan, each stride moving him feet closer to his escape from this annoying school.

"Hey! Drew, but it doesn't matter." It was Sin calling him.

He paused, aggravated that he was no longer on his escape route. He turned to look at the girl realizing that this was a good thing. One of his projects for the day was being presented to him. "Where were you today?"

Sin let a smile cross over her pudgy face. The white makeup was globbing up around her hairline where she had begun to sweat allowing her tanned skin to shine through. "You expected me to go to school? Really? I was skipping, genius." She stood in silence looking at the fake Drew as if she was sizing him up. "Wanna go get some pizza?"

Major Wallace did not respond. He just got into his car and unlocked the passenger door. The gesture wasn't lost on Sarah. She walked around the car and let herself in.

The drive to Pepperoni Pals was a quiet one. Major Wallace had trouble concentrating, his brain filled with adolescent garbage that suddenly seemed to matter to him too much.

They arrived and silently went into the restaurant ordering their pizza by the slice. The sharp aromas of sausages and peppers seemed to help the Major focus again. He sat down at a rickety old chair with his oversized piece of pizza splayed out in front of him. It held the grease of the cheese so evenly that the entire slice glistened under the florescent lighting. He pushed his internal rejection aside and took a bite out of the slice of heart-attack-pie.

Sin smirked at him as if she could see his objections to the food. "There is nothing like the slow suicide of a Pepperoni Pals diet." She slowly opened her mouth to eat her own pizza. The act sent off confused vibes somewhere between gothic angst and seductive slut.

Reminding himself to get back into character with the brooding hatred of humanity, Major Wallace spoke out in Drew's squeaky voice, "It doesn't have the same poetic justice as the filth they feed us in school. To think something is so vile, so destructive to our bodies and we are forced to pay for it both in taxes and at the counter."

"Your own fault for going to class and eating the slop they shove in front of you. I choose my demise, you are just following orders." She turned and spit on the floor showing her disgust for the boy's choices.

Major Wallace shuddered at her comment of

following orders. It was as if she knew who he was, a soldier as opposed to the teenager he wanted to appear as. He only let the thought settle for a brief moment before he brushed into the void of lost memories.

A glass fell in the kitchen leaving the echoes of shattering dinnerware throughout the restaurant. The Major almost did not even notice the sound as he was beginning to pay close attention to Sin.

"No one worth impressing is struck by conformity, by attending class, and by doing what you're supposed to do."

The words were sinking into the military man as he sat across from her stuffing his face with the grotesque food. He began to think that she was right. If he was going to make a good life for Drew to return to, maybe he should be rebelling a bit more.

"At least you aren't being the band nerd snitch anymore." She smiled as her black lipstick cracked showing her lush red lips below.

Major Wallace, stupefied, nodded in agreement with the girl.

She stood up pushing her chair back into the aisle. "Think about it. Life can be so much better." She raised her pointer finger to her mouth biting hard on the skin. She pierced the flesh allowing a small droplet of blood to pool on the tip. Taking two steps to round the table, Sin knelt down in front of Major Wallace. She held her finger out in front of his face. Tracing the air in front of him from his forehead down to his mouth, she kept her bloody appendage just millimeters from his skin.

Regardless of how seductive and dark she meant for the action to be, all Major Wallace could think was 'don't touch me, don't touch me. I will give you anything you want just don't touch me'.

She smiled and stuck her finger into her mouth laughing at the taste of her own blood. She stood and walked away swinging her hips as if Drew was watching.

Major Wallace let out a sigh of relief thinking how lucky he was she did not touch him.

As Sin opened the door to leave the pizza joint, she shouted back at Drew, "Don't worry so much. I was never planning on touching you. But, now that you will give me anything, you will be my escort." She laughed deep and dark as the door shut behind her.

Major Wallace turned around in terror to see the girl donning a venomous look. But all he could do was mutter, "Did I say that out loud?"

TWELVE

ACROPHOBIA GETS YOU HIGH

Major Wallace sat in Drew's room still reeling from the events of the day. His questions about Sin were becoming more serious. He was pretty sure she read his mind, which he could deal with, but he was starting to believe his juvenile thoughts throughout the day may have been planted in his brain. If she was putting thoughts in his head, he might be in trouble.

The clock changed to nine p.m. and Major Wallace closed his eyes in a futile attempt at relaxation before his briefing. The aromas of the room focused the man as he opened his eyes to the sight of General Pounder standing before him.

"All right soldier. Let me have it. Full briefing, now!" The general was in no mood for delays.

Major Wallace turned his body to get off the bed and stand at attention. He stared past the General and his massive form, which seemed to overcrowd the room, and began his report.

"Physical transition has been coming along fine. There is now a noticeable change in the amount of muscle on the body. The switch should go unnoticed by the civilians in Private Darby's life. The small yet noticeable changes such as haircut and complexion changes have already been taken care of. The behavioral transition…"

General Pounder interrupted Major Wallace's report, "Major, I will assume you have accomplished the menial. I want to know about the energivore."

Major Wallace silently shuddered at the thought of talking about the day. "Sin appears to be more advanced than I thought. She has developed some psychic abilities beyond her natural energy sucking. I believe she has read my mind and possibly planted some thoughts in my brain as well."

He wanted to duck from the tirade he assumed was to follow. To his surprise General Pounder seemed to be expecting the news. "You need to keep a close eye on her. She may be in league with Lucky, but there is not too much at risk since we have him locked up right now. If you think she has acquired any classified information from reading your thoughts you need to apprehend her and bring her in as soon as possible." The General looked around the room mulling over his decision. "Don't worry about filing the rest of the report. With an energivore out there, we don't need to focus on the transition. I expect you will do your job without constant supervision."

The general dissolved away into the air before the last word had hit Major Wallace's ear. He sat back down on the bed running ideas through his head of how he could possibly apprehend Sarah. If it had been anyone else, anyone who was not a shape shifter, it would just have been a matter of getting her cuffed. That was not the case for Major Wallace. How could he capture someone he couldn't touch?

His body felt shaky and his stomach went nervous. He paced the room trying to calm himself when a realization hit him. General Pounder, who was known for losing his temper, barely reacted to the news that Sin seemed to be a mind reader, even after reporting he only thought she had done it. He could have mumbled his fear of her touching him; she may not be as advanced as he was claiming. It may all be a coincidence.

A couple of deep breaths soothed his nerves and he lay down on the bed. As he tried to give his body and mind over to slumber he told himself he needed to be sure that Sin was doing what he thought. He needed to give her another chance. The last thing he wanted to do was capture an innocent civilian and put her in front of a military judge.

FOURTEEN

JANUARY IS THE RETURN TO CLASS

The shiny blob flew past Sam's head as he tried to take cover behind a rock. There were no clear shots. He could not possibly hit the enemy from his current position. He looked to his side to see Drew hiding in a foxhole spending too much time trying to generate some psi. "Dude! Stop worrying about the attacks. I will fend them off - you figure out how to get into the base. There are only two of them left so it shouldn't be that hard."

Drew looked over, letting the psi dribble out of his hands and into the dirt he was sitting on. "But there are only two of us too. It's not like we have an advantage here." Drew panicked. He felt lost with his lack of ability for psi generation, especially in the middle of a battle.

"Just read their thoughts!" Sam was getting aggravated. He leaned to the side past the rock and lobbed a large glop of psi hitting one of the soldiers. "There, now there is only one of them. Go capture their flag!"

Drew collected himself and searched for the mind of

his fellow soldier. He did not understand the interest the other boot campers found in the game. It just seemed like a pointless endeavor to play silly battle games with their fellow soldiers.

He found the thoughts of the other boy. The boy knew where Drew was located and he was heavily covered from Sam's attacks. His intentions were to stay covered and pick off Drew and Sam as they tried to maneuver toward his flag. Drew was a sitting duck the second he moved out of his foxhole.

Drew looked over at the drill sergeant, the grey haired one who also happened to be his psi generation teacher, in an attempt to figure out if they were running out time for the game. There was no sign the drill sergeant was intending on leaving before someone won the capture the flag game. He may not have cared for the game, but it was better than the normal physical training of pushups and mile long runs.

Drew came up with a plan. He looked over at Sam and whispered, "When he gets distracted come out running." Sam nodded as if he understood what Drew was talking about. Drew took a deep breath, got to his feet and leapt out of the foxhole. The kid across the way saw him and peered out of his hiding place to get a good shot of psi at Drew. He headed straight for the edge of the camp, away from his opponents' flag.

Drew's heart pounded, his mind raced faster than his feet, the quietness of the battle ringing in his ears. It was a surprise that Drew was in no physical danger yet his body was teeming with adrenaline. Drew shot a quick glance to his left to see the kid holding his hands straight out in front of him preparing to release a barrage of the shiny purple goo. The psi came flying through the air and Drew jumped with every bit of energy he had.

His body fell to the ground just behind the drill sergeant leading the psi to splatter all over the teacher. The grey haired man took a deep breath and let his rage control his eyes. His skin puffed up as his color went from a fleshy pink to a feverish red.

The boy who shot the psi panicked and ran over to apologize before being sentenced to hours of pushups. Sam saw the opportunity and sprinted for the flag. Drew had wanted to shoot the kid, but he was also hit with the psi that was deflected off the drill sergeant and according to the rules that meant he was out of the game.

The boy reached the drill sergeant with his blubbery apology just as Sam grasped the wooden pole that held the flag. Sam was the sole survivor of his team and the game winner.

The drill sergeant looked at the kid, accidently letting a burst of laughter leave his lips. He composed himself and congratulated Sam and Drew for their ingenuity. Everyone got to their feet and wiped the psi off their clothes. Out of the dozen soldiers who played in the game, the blond haired girl and the grey haired drill sergeant did not come clean. Although they did not notice, their uniforms continued to shine of the purple-y substance as they made their way back to the heart of the base.

Drew walked behind the girl who he had accidently fantasized over staring at the purple-y substance still clinging to her body. Reminding himself that psi was the manifestation of intention and purpose, he thought about the possibility that the blond haired girl and the grey haired drill sergeant were having some kind of inappropriate affair. Or, maybe one of them intended to. He had already seen psi land upon the two of them in psi generation class. There was something there. He just was not sure what it was.

When they arrived back at the brightness of the camp they dutifully went to OBE class. Drew was never completely at ease in OBE class or remote viewing for that matter. He felt that he was not as talented at the disciplines as the USAPO seemed to think he was.

The drill sergeant stood at the front of the room looking like a clone of ninety-nine percent of the officers at the camp. "Soldiers, welcome back. By this point, you should all have been able to experience an OBE. We only have a few days left of weapons training in OBE and you all need to have experienced the sensation before you leave me. Now let me see the hands of those who have not yet achieved an OBE."

Drew was the only hand in the air, attempting to retreat once he realized how uncommon his failure seemed to be.

"Alright then. Private Darby, I need you come sit in the chair here in the front of the class. We will not be leaving today until you achieve Out-Of-Body!" The military Sergeant tapped on the chair at the front of the room with a mix of excitement and frustration.

Drew, not wanting to aggravate the instructor any more, got up from his seat to go take his place in display of the rest of the class. The walk was humiliating as he scanned the room for thoughts of jest, possible taunts to his psyche. There were none, mostly thoughts of boredom and annoyance that they had to sit and be unproductive.

Drew sat down in the chair and listened to the drill sergeant as he explained exactly what to do.

"I want you to close your eyes. Keep perfectly still with your hands on your lap, feet on the floor." Drew followed the instructions with little effort. "Focus on your feet. Feel the blood drain out of them. Feel your feet begin to tingle and as the sensation fades picture your feet fading away so your body is left with stumps at the end of your legs." Drew again followed the instruction, but suddenly his mind filled with thoughts of Cerberus guarding the center of the base.

He could not focus on his nerves anymore as he could almost hear the screaming of the beings inside the gates of Hell being watched over by the demonic hounds.

"Private Darby! Focus!" The drill sergeant stared deep into the boy looking for his thoughts. "Who is doing that?" The instructor seemed worried about the thoughts he could see inside Drew.

"Sorry sir, I seem to be having trouble focusing." Drew let the words squeak out his mouth losing the force of his recently acquired military speech.

"No, those thoughts you are having are being implanted. You have not learned that skill yet." He paused for a moment and looked out into the class. "Who is doing that?" He seemed genuinely disturbed by the situation. He turned his attention back to Drew. "Just put up a blocker."

Drew stared up at the man with confusion scrawled across his face and radiating from his thoughts.

Obviously frustrated with Drew's lack of knowledge he explained. "Imagine a clear box over your head." Drew immediately remembered the grey haired drill sergeant telling him the same thing. He did as he was told and the stereotypical military man shouted, "Ten hours!"

Drew's thoughts became clear again and he closed his eyes, focusing on his feet. He allowed the sensation of the tingling to drop away as did his feet in his mind's vision. He continued allowing different body parts to fade away as their nerves appeared to go dead with his thoughts.

"Now you should be nothing but a floating head. Gather all of your emotions, your thoughts, and your existence and focus it to your forehead just above your brow ridge."

The instructions should have baffled Drew, but after envisioning his body fading into darkness somehow the idea made sense. He pushed all of his being into a small point on his skull. A tremendous pressure came down upon Drew's actual face almost pulling him out of the trance he was in.

"Now push it out. Force your mind out of your third

eye and out into the room."

He pushed.

The room came into focus as Drew stood looking at the class, assuming he had failed and just stood up. The drill sergeant was not looking at him and class had not reacted to his vertical position. He slowly turned around to see his body relaxed in the chair with a small silver strand coming out his head pulled taught to where he was standing. The fear of what he was seeing was a sensation that nearly pulled him back into his body. It was similar to when Major Wallace appeared in his barracks disguised as Drew. There was just something about seeing yourself from another perspective.

He looked around the room feeling slightly different from normal, the air more crisp, and his body slightly lighter. He felt somewhat off kilter.

Looking around the room, he could see psi emanating off each person, each a slightly different color, almost as if it represented their moods. The blond haired girl looking annoyed had a red tint to her psi. It was also a grayish gold, but a bit of black was stuck to her forehead. He looked over at Sam who was gushing with pure white psi.

He turned to look his own body to see what he was seeping, but something else caught his eye. Flying high within in the room was what appeared to be a girl with a man in tow. It was a chubby darkly tanned girl who screeched by in a near blur of colors. Behind her she looked to be dragging a man in a military uniform. He couldn't see the features as they seemed to be shifting constantly.

Drew thought the girl looked familiar, but could not place her. She dropped the normal purple psi as she flew through the wall of the building and out of sight. He watched the psi as it fell and peered on in amazement as the shining goo formed letters and pictures.

It was a very discernable 'USAPO' followed by what Drew could only assume was a skull and crossbones. Just the sight of it brought chills to him. As the rest of the psi fell, it began to form into an orange horseshoe, but before Drew could fully detect what the message was the drill sergeant slapped Drew on the back. He went screaming through the air pulled by the silver cord attached to the head of his spirit.

He slammed back into his body with a thud causing him to gasp for air.

The drill sergeant let smile paint his face. "With a reaction like that, it is safe to assume you have now reached OBE. Haven't had a failed student yet."

That was the end of the class, but Drew was uneasy. He could only assume that the USAPO stood for United States Army Psychic Operations. Just seeing the skull and crossbones next to it worried him. Adding to that, the idea there were gates which seemed to be guarded by Cerberus, the three-headed hound of Hell, Drew was downright worried about the safety of his soul.

FIFTEEN

COST PER NIGHT, BUSINESS OF A HOTEL

The world seemed to be crashing around Drew. He felt the proof was mounting that he was in league with an evil organization. What was worse, that evil organization was a group that belonged to one of the most noble efforts in the free world, or so he thought.

After returning to the barracks, Drew did not speak to Sam. He did not want to worry him. Sam had wanted this for so long and he was so excited to be a part of it, but he couldn't see the psi the way Drew did. Nobody did for some reason. At least that realization made him feel more successful than he had felt recently.

Drew lay in bed nervous about his future, his life, and his soul. Sleep was not going to be possible tonight, so he tried to achieve OBE again.

Eyes closed. The sensations filled his legs, his arms, his chest and one by one they faded into nothingness. The process was simpler the second time. The only difference was that he did not need to force his existence out through his forehead; instead he simply sat up and rose out of his body. It seemed to be a gentler way to exit his physical self.

Once he was out of his body he walked straight out of the room, relieved to be stepping away from this wicked place. He wished he did not remain there physically, but at least he was not consciously experiencing it.

He walked out the door and out onto the base. He could hear the growling of Cerberus and he knew it was directed toward him. It was as if the hound could tell Drew had figured out the army's relation to evil. Drew wanted nothing to do with it and he walked away from the base into the darkness of the cave.

Even in his spirit form all the light faded away. Before he knew it he was walking into an emptiness that felt like it was infinite. Unfortunately, the black abyss he was heading toward felt less lonely than the base he had just come from.

Drew turned back to make sure the silver cord was still attached and he hadn't walked away from physical life. The line, the only thing he could see in the darkness was still attached. It was a safety net of sorts. He was pretty sure he could pull that cord and be yanked back into his body.

When he turned back to the nothingness he noticed some psi off in the distance. The shimmer of the purple phantom goo twinkled the tiniest bit of hope into his forlorn heart.

The psi was forming an escalator. It was the same area he had seen the day they descended into this Hell. He thought maybe it was his ticket out. He went toward it and followed it up. He ascended the hill hoping to feel the heaviness of the evil he was leaving lift up and unburden him, but it didn't happen. It felt like it was attached to him, following him everywhere he went.

Up the escalator he went until he suddenly walked out of the mountain. He was in the desert alone, in the cold of night. The moon overhead left a slight blue tint to the world. Reception battalion could be seen in the distance, but other than that it was just him and nature.

He turned back to see the mountain. The rock itself looked solid, but he knew there was an invisible entrance in the notch of the mountain he had just emerged from. A faint hint of psi covered the mountain. He assumed it was negative as most the psi he'd seen had been so. But there was that small bit of doubt that entered his mind that maybe it was not so bad. The idea that maybe he was wrong about the military, a thought that came from somewhere familiar, but not from where most of his thoughts had been originating recently. It was almost as if it was a more natural thought.

Before he could spend any time contemplating this, his mind was invaded by ferocious visions. He saw death and famine, bodies being burnt alive, and women being killed in their homes. His nostrils filled with the scent of mortality while his knees gave out sending dull echoing pains through his legs. He tried to push the visions out, but they just became stronger. Finally, he saw Mr. Harkins, his manager at HappyLand, standing in his full military garb. However, instead of the American flag stitched to the arm of his uniform, there was an inverted pentagram.

Drew gasped trying to fill his spiritual lungs, but nothing happened except another barrage of sensations of the terror of the military. He could not open his eyes. He could not find the silver cord to pull him back to his body. He turned back to the direction he knew the mountain to be and scrambled back. After a few feet the vision subsided.

He opened his eyes to see nothing, darkness. He was back inside the mountain still thinking about the evil in the camp, but the traumatizing visions were gone. Drew, now seeing the silver line, tugged on it and shot back into his physical body.

He opened his eyes, still lying on his bunk. He worried about things infiltrating his mind. He felt he was going insane. He put up the only defense he knew of; he did the blocker trick with the invisible box over his head. He whispered, "Ten hours."

All the thoughts of evil and the military faded into memories and all he was left thinking was maybe he was wrong about the military being evil. After all, the frightening visions only appeared after he was away from Fort Inspire. But then again maybe it was a deterrent to going AWOL. He could not be sure. All he knew was that his mind felt clear finally and maybe he could get some sleep.

SIXTEEN

FEBRUARY, WELL IT DEPENDS ON WHERE

Major Wallace finished his jog and walked back into the house. He got a hug from Drew's father as he walked out the door to go to work. The hugs in the house were something that Major Wallace had not gotten used to. At least none of the Darbys were energivores. The hugs were not exhausting, only uncomfortable.

He grabbed his bags and said his farewells to his temporary mother and headed off to school. He drove through the normal bumper to bumper traffic on the three-mile trek arriving at his usual time, parking in his usual spot, and following his usual schedule.

He had almost completed two weeks at the school. The morning classes were Physics and band before lunchtime. Band was a class that Major Wallace dreaded as he was not as musically inclined as Drew, but he only had it twice a week so he forced his way through.

On his way into the massive bricked building, he spotted Daisy out of the corner of his eye. He was worried about accomplishing his promise of making Drew popular, but he thought he might be able to patch things up a bit with his dream girl.

"Daisy!" Major Wallace called out in his Drew voice as he trotted toward the young girl. She looked back in disgust hitting him with thoughts of disgust as she glanced at the scar on her hand. Wallace called out again attempting to ignore her thoughts which were pounding his brain. "Wait up, I just want to say something."

Daisy paused clenching her teeth. Why would Drew Darby want to speak to her when he hadn't said a word to her in five years, maybe longer? She stood in place gluing her feet to the pavement. She turned back as she heard his steps slow nearing her.

"Hey Daisy, I just…" The fake Drew trailed off as the girl interrupted him.

"What?" She leaned forward a bit and glared into his eyes. Something turned her stomach, something offset her. "Stay away from me. You are not the same person I used to know." She did not know what it was, but she knew it was something she did not want to be a part of. Something in Drew, and it shook her core being.

Major Wallace could not hold back the flood of emotions the girl was feeling and he retreated into the school. A few minutes after entering the doors, the first bell rang to let the students know they only had five minutes to get to class before they were tardy. Major Wallace sauntered through the hallways saying hi to a couple of people who did not seem to dislike Drew as much as the rest.

He made it into Physics just moments before the tardy bell. He took his seat and stared out the window by the door. The teacher began his boring speech about vectors and the direction of momentum, sedating the class as usual.

While peering out into the hallway, Sin broke his stare when she came up to the glass. Looking into the room for him, she motioned for Drew to get up and leave class. She waved her hand asking him to come followed by the rocker devil horns hand symbol, trying to convince him it would be more fun than class.

Major Wallace shrugged it off as if to say, I'm already here, might as well stay. He was conducting an experiment at the same time. He wanted to make sure one more time to see if she was a mind reader. So, as he waved and brooded for her benefit as his audience, he also put in his mind that he would skip class if she waited ten more minutes.

He looked her in the face and nodded while he imagined the clock ticking ten minutes more hoping he was not giving anything away in his face. He glanced at the clock, but when he returned his attention to the door Sin was walking away. She had given up on him.

He watched her walk down the hallway seeing her newly re-dyed black hair brush against her tanned skin badly covered in white powdered base. As she turned the corner, he saw a teacher speed walking down the hall as if she had something of great importance ahead. It was an odd sight, but Major Wallace ignored it and refocused on the Physics lesson, which was beneath his caliber of thought.

Eventually class let out and he wandered out into the hallway, enjoying being a kid again. He looked for Sin between classes but she was nowhere to be found. Assuming she had given up and skipped class alone, he went on to band class.

He wandered in a bit late which the director ignored and he sat in his chair holding his tuba and pretended to play. It was a couple hours of excruciating boredom. Major Wallace wanted nothing more than get up and walk out, but that was not his job. His job was to keep Drew's life intact.

He suffered through the class, but as the bell rang, the band director called Drew and asked him to stay after class. Major Wallace's heart sank, but he did as requested.

"Is something wrong Drew? Anything at home that you want to talk about?" The band director posed the questions with exceedingly soothing tones.

Wallace realized that he had alerted too many people that he was acting odd. It was an unexpected development for him as he usually was an excellent replacement for recruits. "I am sorry sir."

"It's ok Drew, but I just have been a little concerned. You haven't stopped by in the mornings to help out in the halls and you haven't been taking your instrument home." He looked at Drew with true concern.

Major Wallace suddenly realized he had been manipulated, not by the band director, but by someone else. This man had the same thoughts and concerns for Drew as the other teacher had, but for some reason this man did not annoy Major Wallace. He had been acting juvenile often while at school and making stupid mistakes in his mimicry of Drew's behaviors. It had to be Sarah.

Major Wallace centered his attention on the band director. "I am sorry sir, I just want to have more friends. People don't like me getting them in trouble in the mornings and I just..." Major Wallace suddenly had become the Drew he should have been the entire time.

The band director let out a sigh of relief. "Don't worry about it Drew. It's fine, I can handle the band hall myself." He gave the boy a smile and a pat on the shoulder. "Why don't you come to the band dance this weekend? I think you would be surprised how inviting the rest of the band can be."

"Sure. I'll do that," Major Wallace said as he got up to leave. Two birds with one stone. Go to the dance, convince everyone he was acting normal and make a few friends while he was at it.

The band director watched Drew mosey over to the door when he added, "I almost forgot." He paused as Drew turned back to look at him. "Be careful with that girl you've been hanging around. I have seen you talking to her in the parking lot. She isn't a student here. She was chased off campus earlier today by a teacher on their conference period."

Major Wallace suddenly realized that was why he was thinking so clearly now. Sin was too far away. "Don't worry sir. I know she's not who she claims to be." And with that, he headed toward the parking lot.

SEVENTEEN

IT IS ALL UP TO YOU

Major Wallace felt that he had accomplished something as he walked out of the school toward the parking lot. There were a few people who nodded, giving polite waves to him. It was not the popularity he had promised Drew, but it was a start.

As he walked out the doors of the school, the warm air of spring hit him dead in the face. It was as if he had walked into a sauna without the humidity. As he stepped out into the hot sunlight, the dry air burned off the chill that the air conditioners had given his skin.

He scanned the lot for his hatchback. He spotted it in the same spot as always, but any walk in the high temperatures was too far. He put on an annoyed face to blend back in and walked out into the heat on his way to his car.

The normal sounds of afterschool were floating around him - car horns, kids yelling, the patter of feet across the pavement... It nearly put him in a trance. He was so zoned out he nearly missed Sin yelling at him from across the street. He looked up to see the girl in her usual gothic clothes standing in a clearing at the edge of a neighborhood. It was called the smoking spot as the kids in school used it as a place to vape when they skipped class.

She waved her arms madly bouncing her hefty frame up and down as she screamed, "Come pick me up! I wanna hang out! Go to the mall!"

Major Wallace was far from excited about the prospect of going to the mall. After all, he disliked the amount of time he was surrounded by kids at school; the mall was just an extension of that torture. However, it was not his decision; his career required him to go. He would not succeed in his mission without spending more time with the gothic student impersonator.

As he got into his little vehicle, he wondered why he had not realized it earlier. He had only seen her in school once before, she always wanted him to 'skip class' with her, and she looked much too old to be in high school. It seemed obvious now. The question was, why was she befriending Major Wallace?

He drove out of the parking lot and around the corner to pick her up. He leaned over and unlocked her door.

She plopped down into the passenger seat and started talking immediately, "Today was a waste of existence. The dregs of society tried to destroy my identity."

Wallace had no idea what she was talking about and unless it revealed more about her abilities, he did not care. "What do you want to do at the mall?" He purposefully interrupted her hoping to bring her out of the gothic tirade.

"Oh. I need some new clothes and I want you to meet my friend." She peered out the window as they made short trip to the local mall. "I think the two of you could really get it on." She laughed at her crude remark.

The rest of the ride was silent. Major Wallace could feel his thoughts turning dark and immature. He took it as proof that Sin was incorporating some kind of mind control over him. It showed her abilities impressive since he had a military grade protection kept about him at all times, as did all members of the military. It was put in place while the soldier, sailor, marine, or airman was sworn in. Anyone who could get past that kind of protection was someone to be wary of.

When they arrived at the mall, Sin jumped out of the car and shouted at 'Drew' to come along as she sprinted toward the building. It was an average mall, nothing special in any way. Major Wallace tucked away this revelation as another reason Drew Darby's life was lackluster at best.

He walked at his normal speed through the cracked old parking lot up to the entrance. As soon as he placed his foot upon the spit stained walkway he heard two screams that reminded him of tires squealing.

He looked up to find Sin in the middle of an embrace with a tall dark haired girl. The two spun in circles continuing the rouse of being of school age. The sight was odd. Sin and her average height and slightly wide frame was turning in circles with a girl nearly twice her height and hair color as dark as Sin's new dye job. Their oversized black clothes spun into a whirlwind of fabric and chains as if they had suddenly become a two-headed gothic monster. They finally parted and the new girl backed up to take in the sight of Major Wallace.

She cracked a huge smile revealing her revolting teeth. Some went sideways, some seemed to be missing, and a few looked like they were growing behind one another. It was as if someone had put a blender in her mouth.

Major Wallace tried not to react to the hideousness of Sarah's friend, but he was not sure if he accomplished his goal.

The two girls turned and headed into the sliding glass doors of the mall motioning for Wallace to tag along.

He followed obediently as he had learned to do while in the military. The doors opened as he stepped close and the air conditioning brought his focus to the surface. It felt like entering a different planet. The place was surprisingly dark even though there were lights and skylights in the ceiling. Everyone was milling around looking to spend money trying to enhance the superficiality of their lives through the lights of progress.

He followed the girls down a hallway and down an escalator giving Major Wallace the grim feeling they were entering a deep cavern that rarely allowed those who noticed to escape.

He noticed that the thoughts of the customers around him were completely self-absorbed. There were no thoughts of others, of charity, of compassion... All that filled the air was obsession and wantonness. It really began to get to him when he passed a toy store and the corrupt ideas had seeped into the children, commonly the most pure of thought.

The girls giggled like children as they went into a store and started to look at swimsuits. Major Wallace could feel his mind growing more and more childish as he looked at the girls holding up the skimpy underwear not able to keep his mind trained on important issues.

"Sorry, Drew. This is Peccadillo. She is homeschooled, but she is as bad as anyone you've ever met." Sin finally acknowledged the meeting of her two 'friends'.

Peccadillo ran a tongue across her top lip, smearing a bit of the cheap black lipstick that covered it. She let her disgusting grill show as she reached out to shake Drew's hand.

Major Wallace feigned shyness to avoid touching the friend of the energivore, just in case. He dodged back behind a clothing rack giving a verbal salutation instead.

He watched the two girls pretend to be younger than they were reminding him of a teen drama where all the actors are in their thirties, but the characters are in high school. He thought that as a trio they were all trying to fake out someone.

The girls sauntered into a dressing room together giggling and attempting to force Major Wallace into an adolescent stupor.

"Come here." Peccadillo called through the thin plywood dressing room door.

Major Wallace, focusing on being an adult, made his way over to the room the two girls were changing in. He stared at the ground as the girls spoke to him through the wall.

Sin piped up, "There is a party on Saturday. We think you would enjoy yourself." She put emphasis on the end of her sentence to derail his mind to innuendo.

Peccadillo joined in. "I would love for you," She paused, "to come." Again, the emphasis hit hard the last two words. The girls giggled at their puns.

Major Wallace realized that it was opposite the dance, not that he wanted to go to that either, but he was going to be torn between keeping an eye on Sin and convincing everyone Drew was acting normal.

"Please." Sin let the word out with a pathetic whine.

Major Wallace thought to himself, 'assuming you aren't incarcerated by the USAPO by that time.' He chuckled to himself before answering aloud. "Sure, why not."

There was no response. Major Wallace looked up between the crack in the door and the wall of the dressing room. The girls must have read his mind about the incarceration, because they both looked shocked.

Major Wallace was about to look down again when something grabbed his attention. He risked sliding the door open just a crack to get a good look. The two girls were standing in the room topless, but that was not what caught his eye. It was a very apparent aura around Peccadillo. It was not a normal aura of bright colors, but a dark dense aura, pitch black, held together by lost souls and demons.

Major Wallace knew what that was. It was not the aura of a demon or an energivore, but the aura of a human being, possessed by pure evil.

EIGHTEEN

MAY I, YOU CAN

Drew and Sam rounded the corner of the building in the center of camp. Drew still felt chills as he passed by the steel structure almost hearing the bark of the Hell hound. He felt the intensity of the beast shake his psyche. It was as if he was being stalked by insanity, and he could not handle it any longer.

Drew ignored the path they were to take on the physical training run and yanked Sam around a corner pulling him behind a building.

"What the Hell? Why did you do that?" Sam was flabbergasted at Drew's action.

"I have to tell you something." Drew took deep breaths worried about Sam's reaction. He closed his eyes and dove in headfirst. "I think the military may be evil."

An eyebrow cocked on Sam's face. "Really?" There were no regal words for his confusion. There was nothing but a common utterance to explain his perception of Drew's thoughts.

Drew sank down against the building realizing the idiocy of his statement, but there was more to it. How could he explain everything to Sam?

Sam kept an eye on his friend as the rest of his body slowly drifted back toward their running route.

"I am not crazy, dude. Look, while I was in the OBE during class, I saw some things." Drew stared at the concrete under his feet as if he wasn't even talking to Sam.

The way Drew formed the words grabbed Sam's attention. He wanted to hear more, but they needed to keep moving unless they wanted to get in trouble. "That could be serious, but right now we need to get back to the barracks, because I don't want to do pushups for the next twelve hours."

Drew understood; after all, he would suffer the same fate if he stayed there. He got to his feet and the boys sprinted off through the camp hoping they would still make it back in time.

Major Wallace turned off the alarm. It was thirty minutes earlier than he normally had it set. But he needed the emergency briefing and this was the only time General Pounder could set aside for the Major.

Major Wallace sat up in bed and realizing that he was slightly behind schedule, he rolled out of the bed to get dressed. He barely got his shirt buttoned before the General appeared in the room.

The waft of the air, the movement of his shadow, the swaying of the light all stopped as General Pounder froze time. "This better be important Major. REPORT!"

Major Wallace wasted no time with nervous hesitation. "I have come to the conclusion that Sarah also known as Sin is a potentially dangerous energivore. She knows her abilities and has some very powerful mind control techniques that she has used on me."

The General grunted as he heard the news.

"She has a friend who goes by the name of Peccadillo. She appears possessed by some dark forces. She is plainly human, but her aura has been overridden by shadows. Together they appear to be attempting to lure me to some kind of party, I do not know what the reason is. I have the feeling they know I am not Drew Darby." Major Wallace took a breath.

"Bring them to the Psychic Opeations basic training facilities. We will question them and put them in the brig." Pounder said, authoritative and to the point. He turned to teleport out of the room.

Major Wallace risked the insubordination. "Is that the best plan of action? We do not know if they are in league with Lucky."

The General turned ever so slowly, mostly for effect. He gazed his humongous eyes into the soul of the Major. His voice came out soft in an almost whisper. "Evil is evil. Just because they may not be involved with Lucky doesn't mean they are not enemies of the United States. It doesn't mean they aren't evil. It doesn't mean they need to be on the loose." He paused as he turned his back again. "Do whatever you have to do. Use whoever you have to use. Spend anything you have to spend, but bring them both in within twenty-four hours!" He vanished into the background.

Major Wallace fell back onto the bed regretting doing what had to be done. He thought for a moment on how he could apprehend the girls. He had only one plan. Only one man could help him, but it was time to get ready for school.

Drew lay down on his bunk. It had been a hard day. It had been a long day or maybe he just was worn out from not trusting his superiors anymore. But it was night time and Drew could finally fill in Sam on all of his visions.

Sam waited patiently. He did not ask Drew anything, but he refused to lie down unless Drew was asleep. He would not miss any information Drew offered up on his own.

"Have you noticed anything strange about the building at the center of camp?"

Sam had not expected a question. He wanted a full confession from Drew of what he was seeing. "Ummm. Yeah, it is kinda creepy."

"I had a dream about three dogs guarding it. Then every time I get near it I can sense them there."

"It is probably your mind playing tricks on you." Sam was trying to be comforting, but he felt also uneasy around that building.

"No, it's more than that. I believe the dogs I saw are a mythical creature called Cerberus."

Sam piped up offering the quick synopsis he remembered from school. "Right, the dog that guards the gates of Hell." The realization hit him. If those were the gates of Hell, then they were bunking with the Devil's mountainside view.

The boys went back and forth, but after Drew explained all of his experiences, Sam was not arguing anymore. They were both suddenly terrified.

NINETEEN

HE JUST WANTS TO WATCH

Major Wallace ran through his normal routine. He showered, went for a jog, and ate breakfast. His mind raced with ways to apprehend the girls, but his body just continued to go through the motions.

He quickly concluded that he felt better skipping school and going straight to the capture of the girls. Of course, he had to be careful not to alert anyone that Drew was acting odd again.

He went into the kitchen where his mother and father were finishing their breakfast. Major Wallace had never paid close attention to either of Drew's parents and in order to carry out his plan he would have to get to know one of them a bit better.

Drew's father gave both of them a hug and headed to his car. That made up Wallace's mind. He would have to connect with Drew's mom, Wendy.

"Aren't you going to be late for school, hon?" She asked with pure innocence in her intention.

"I am usually early anyway. I just wanted to chat with you for a bit." Major Wallace really just wanted her to talk. "What will you be doing today at work? You never really talk about work you know."

His mother took a deep breath in preparation to explaining her work to her son. It seemed odd and she expected it was an attempt to avoid school, but he was a good kid and she did not want to suspect the worst. She spent the next five minutes feeling as though she were being interviewed for a new job. She talked of her responsibilities and her projects and in the end, Drew did not seem any more interested.

"Thanks, mom. I gotta get going or I won't make it to class on time." He gave her a quick hug and peck on the cheek and he rushed out the door. His books were lying on the back seat waiting for use, but today would not be the day. He drove away from the house and went around a couple blocks, parking his car. He looked around to make sure no one was watching him, and he tried to assume the form of Drew's mother.

His body slowly morphed away from the body of the teenaged Drew and into Wendy's middle aged body. The tight skin gave a little slack, the squared frame of Drew gave way to Wendy's curves, and the face aged with frightening speed. It would have been an odd sight, but Major Wallace was reasonably sure no one saw him. He picked up his cell phone and dialed information to get the number for his high school.

Once the phone was connected, he assumed Drew's

mother's voice and called himself in sick for the day. It seemed a much more elaborate plan than it turned out to be. He shook his body and returned to his Drew form.

He drove the hatchback to school. He had to find Sin and Peccadillo, and the school parking lot was where he always ran into Sin.

Even with the delays of the morning, he still got to the parking lot before school started. Parking the car, he looked around for the girls, but they were nowhere to be seen.

He got out and walked around the asphalt lot. He nodded at a couple of people again, hoping to help Drew's lack of friendship. He saw Daisy coming from between a couple of midsized pickups. She appeared to be late, holding a couple of books in her arms and barely keeping them from sprawling out on the ground.

He motioned to her, but her acknowledgment of him was limited to an increase in her pace and a refusal to look him in the eye.

Major Wallace considered that Sin had been run off the other day by law enforcement and maybe she would not return to the campus, so he ventured across the street to the smoking spot, but there was no Sin there either.

He scanned the immediate area for thoughts, he looked for psi that she might have dropped, and he tried everything he could think of before returning to his car to admit defeat.

It was there at his lowest point, when he thought that he might not find her within the General's deadline, that he heard her sarcastic voice call across the lot.

"Drew, but it doesn't matter! You're late for class!" She giggled at his continual determination to go to class.

Major Wallace felt a vapor of relief burn through his body. "Sin! I was looking for you. Wanted to hang out."

"Sounds good, I was waiting for Peccadillo. You want to come along?" She tried to pout her lips and become sultry, but Major Wallace was not falling for it today.

He made his way toward her at the edge of the parking lot when Peccadillo pulled up in a shimmering new BMW. She parked it on the street and got out to greet Drew and Sin. "Is he coming with us?" There was no surprise in her voice, as if she was expecting it before she arrived.

"Yeah, let's go have some fun by the stream." Sarah was letting a hint of violence into her voice. Something they were planning would not be good for Major Wallace.

Peccadillo reached out and grabbed Major Wallace's wrist trying to playfully pull him to the car. The second her skin hit his, a searing burn shot through Major Wallace's arm. It was the pain that only accompanied a person possessed against their will.

He had planned to bring help, but the time to do it was right then. The adventure the two girls wanted Major Wallace to go on was a bad road for him, one that may dead end in death or slavery. He thought fast.

"Hey, I gotta piss. I'll be back out in just a minute. Then we'll head out alright?" He was backing up while he was talking. It was unintentional, but he was showing weakness, showing his fear. This may not have been a good move.

He turned and sprinted into the school heading straight for the bathrooms. He could not stop to talk, or get distracted. He entered the musty room, which was already filthy with the grotesque habits of the male youth of the school. He checked the stalls to make sure he was alone. He pulled a pin out of the door hinge and shoved it into the threshold like a doorstopper. One deep breath and then the plan begins.

TWENTY

AUGUST IS ALL ABOUT THE

Sleep was elusive to both Sam and Drew since their discussion earlier about the evil that had been surrounding Drew. They laid in silence on their bunks worried for their lives and souls.

Drew had decided to stop attempting OBE. Although he was interested in finding out more information and clues, he was also afraid that he was vulnerable to his possible enemies in the base camp.

He wondered what the other recruits knew about the intentions of the Psychic Operations. Had anyone else seen any psi around to warn them about the unholy union Drew believed to exist with the military? He could not know. Sam, obviously, was unaware, but what about the others?

What about the blond-haired girl? What about the drill sergeants? Maybe that was the connection between the blond-haired girl and the grey-haired drill sergeant. Maybe they were in cahoots in damning the rest of the soldiers to Hell. Or maybe they were both aware and fighting against it.

Drew let out a sigh in an attempt to let the pressure of the knowledge slip away. It did not. The burden continued to weigh on his conscience. One thing was sure - the blocker box thing helped keep his mind clear, but when it wore off his thoughts were more convoluted than before. Drew tried to put up the blocker only when he was going to class. He let his head swim with confusion while in bed. He thought it was more tolerable than to continually put up the blocker and have to deal with the swarm of thoughts growing larger and larger waiting for him to let his guard down.

The thoughts had died down for the evening. He mostly was stuck in the curiosity of his purpose. He couldn't help but believe he was special. It was almost as if he was the hero prophesized in some ancient text. As if he had infiltrated the enemy and he was destined to rise above it all to be the greatest warrior… But as romantic as the idea sounded it was always followed up with a thought that he might just be in the right place at the right time or maybe he would die a lonely death after the military found out what he knew.

The thoughts would have droned on like this for hours if it was not for Major Wallace appearing in the center of the barracks. A strange fizzing sound demanded the attention of the two boys.

Sam leapt from his bunk, weary of a demon appearing before him. "In the name of God, the son, and the…" He realized it was the Drew clone he had seen a few days prior. "You scared the Hell out of me." He flopped back down on his bed trying not to give away his new found thoughts of demonic soldiers.

Major Wallace ignored the boy and turned to Drew. He still looked just like him. It was almost a mirror image. They both appeared as a fairly lean and fit kid with the short buzzed haircut.

Drew slowly got to his feet worried about the purpose of Major Wallace showing up. Maybe he had read Drew's mind, it wasn't out of the question. It something he himself could accomplish at this point. He cleared his throat and recognized the other him in the room, "Sir?"

Major Wallace was far from pleased with Private Darby's response, but there was no time to adjust the plan. "Private Darby. You are needed in the field."

Drew choked out a laugh at the Major. "I have no training." He was in no mood to give any respect to the superior officer.

"You know enough. The mission is simple and does not require a high level of weapons training." Major Wallace paused, waiting for a response, but received none. He continued, "You will be transporting to your high school where you will apprehend two females and return them to this base."

"Why don't you do it?"

Major Wallace began to think he had not done a good job of imitating Drew, he was obviously more insolent than he had portrayed. "I would, but one is cursed and the other is an energivore. I, as a shape shifter, cannot make physical contact with either of them. You will have to do it."

Drew looked to the ground shaking his head. This was the beginning. The military was going to begin having him apprehend people for false reasons. He knew in his mind that these girls were not evil, it was the military. However, he knew his moral objections were not reason enough for the military to allow him to ignore his new orders. Plus this would get him out of basic and maybe he could find a way out permanently. "Fine."

Major Wallace let a smirk fall onto his face. "Private Darby. I am in a bit of a hole right now, but you need to learn to show respect to your superiors. Right now you should be thrown in the brig just to prove a point. So, watch it Private."

Drew nodded, somewhat shameful of his emotions taking such control of his actions. "I apologize, sir. Are you going to brief me?"

"There is no need. When you transport, I will be implanting all the memories I have created while I was posing as you into your mind. You will instantly recall my experiences as your own. After we get you teleported you will be in the boy's bathroom of your high school just outside the east parking lot. The girls will be waiting for you there."

"Whoa. It's like two a.m. What am I doing inside the school in the middle of the night?"

Major Wallace shuddered at his own plan. How could he trust this boy to bring in two enemies if he was not smart enough to realize the time issues at Fort Inspire? He took a deep breath knowing he had no other options. "Here, in the mountain, the drill sergeants are not telling you the correct time. They are disorienting you so you will be useful during strange hours. So you can run a 23 hour mission and then get two hours of sleep or vice versa."

Drew smiled feeling that he had figured something out. He had not, but he suspected something was off with time inside the base. "Got it. How do I teleport, sir?"

Major Wallace began to disrobe. "Well, first you have to put the right clothes on."

The two soldiers switched to the correct clothing for their current situations.

"Start by visualizing the bathroom at the school."

TWENTY ONE

DECEMBER DISPLAYS FROZEN FOUNTAINS

Drew seemed to be a different person when he appeared inside the locked bathroom. It was as if he had a second chance at life. He looked to each side to get his bearings. The blue porcelain tile of the bathroom made him feel at home. He was disgusted with the lack of respect for cleanliness, but he felt at home nonetheless.

He kicked the pin out from under the door and opened it to the world awaiting him. The browns of the old hallway sent a wave of relief through the boy. He was home. He stepped out into the hallway tempted to go to class and just resume his life as it was before he went into the army, but he knew that plan would not work. He would be captured and put in the brig. He would have to spend the rest of his life with a dishonorable discharge if he was lucky. If he was unlucky they would decide he knew too much. He had no options but to put Major Wallace's plan into action.

He quickly walked down the hallway, avoiding glances from teachers as he remembered Major Wallace's memory of calling him in sick. It would not help him to get caught on campus now. As he approached the doors to the parking lot he saw Daisy walking down the hall.

Suddenly a rush of memories hit him from childhood. Only, it was not his childhood, it was hers. He recalled pushing her down causing a permanent scar to her beautiful hand. He had marred her perfection, he had hurt her, and now he was repulsed by his youthful actions.

Although he could not remember the event from his own mind, he knew that Major Wallace put it in his head so he knew what Daisy felt.

Daisy saw Drew as she turned a corner. She stopped dead in her tracks staring at the boy. There was something different about him, but she couldn't place it. It was as if the boy she knew growing up had returned and the strange man she had spoken to earlier had vanished. She knew it was not true, they were both Drew, but she felt different all of a sudden. She cautiously waved to Drew fearing a response.

Drew tossed his own caution and shouted down the hallway, "I can't talk right now, but I have to say I'm sorry. I just realized what I did to you way back when. And… I am sorry. I am, but I have to go." He dashed out the door of the building leaving the girl stunned in the middle of the hallway holding her hall pass.

He stepped out into the sunlight which struck his face like a hot iron. The pain of the massive power of the light nearly brought the boy to his knees. He stammered as he walked out onto the pavement. Shading his eyes with his hand he peered out into the host of cars to spot two gothic looking girls in the corner of the lot.

It only took two steps before he recognized Sin. He, of course, had Major Wallace's memories of the girls and their behavior, but he had seen this one elsewhere.

Behind all the pale makeup stood the chubby, tanned girl Drew had seen multiple times in his visions at camp. She was the one who had been warning him of the nature of the military. Everything seemed to be too coincidental all of sudden. The girl who was trying to help him was also the person he was sent to apprehend. Something did not feel right.

As he approached the girls, his apprehension grew along with the volume of their giggles. He stamped each step against the hard pavement still squinting from the attack of the sun.

"Drew! I thought you'd never get here." Sin called out to the arriving boy.

He gave them a curious sidelong stare wondering how long Major Wallace had been hiding in the bathroom.

"Hurry up, we want to go." Peccadillo allowed a childish inflection to bounce through her sentence. "Come on." She whined.

He came within a few steps of the girls. "I was just in there for a minute."

Sin grabbed him around the shoulders laughing at his remark. "Let's get out of here." She gave the boy a small shove landing him in the awaiting arms of Peccadillo. He was given a strong hug by the tall girl pressing herself up against him, eliminating any need for imagination.

As they filed into Peccadillo's car the girls giggled with excitement. Three door slams and they were off. Peccadillo drove with Sin and Drew filling up the back seat.

"What I meant was we never thought you, Drew Darby would ever show up. We thought we were going to have to deal with that warring imposter forever, but now you are here. The real Drew Darby." Sin clapped her hands with a joyous fervor.

Drew felt his stomach sink, they knew. He had enacted the plan just minutes before and he had already blown his cover. He sat in silence fearing what was to come.

He watched his town fly by the window of the car. It was the first time he had seen a familiar sight in over a week and he was only able to dread what would happen when the car stopped.

They turned down a private drive off the main road. It was a thin dirt road, barely alive through the invasion of weeds. They drove down for nearly a mile passing a deserted barn to a stream Drew was unaware of.

They got out of the car, Drew felt as though he was facing his mortality. He thought they might be taking him out to pasture.

Peccadillo sat down on a log and patted the old damp wood suggesting Drew keep her company. Sin chuckled to herself feeling the worry within Drew.

Sin looked over at the boy as he made his way to the

fallen tree trunk as if he was a dead man walking. "Relax. We aren't the bad guys."

Drew sat down next to Peccadillo and looked over at Sin inquisitively. "That doesn't necessarily put me at ease."

"There is a world of wonder available to you. You just have to grab it." She paused and watched Peccadillo trace her finger across the boy's chest. "You are one of us and with almost no effort on your part you can have everything you ever wanted. I have a website where I sell random portraits, posters, and statuettes. It brings in tens of thousands monthly. You can be a part of that."

Peccadillo allowed her finger to linger on the nape of Drew's neck. Shivers pooled in his skin breaking his concentration. "But why would you want me? I was a nobody before..." He stopped himself before he revealed his military obligations.

Sin smirked as she turned to look at the stream glistening in the light of the late morning sun. "We take care of our own." She took in a deep breath nearly soothing Drew in the process.

Drew's mind was clouding with confusion. He could not tell if things were making sense anymore. He tried to look for psi, but was inundated with the purple substance in the shapes of coins pouring out of Sin's hands.

He turned toward Peccadillo to see if she was giving off her intentions also, but he was met with a half kiss and a weak pinch from her teeth on his lower lip. Drew relaxed, he couldn't stop the urge.

TWENTY TWO

IF I COULD SUGGEST ONE THING FOR YOU TO DO EVERY DAY, IT WOULD BE TO DANCE

As Drew gave himself to Peccadillo losing all focus he had on the situation, Sin began to speak to him inside his mind. Her voice echoed through the halls of his psyche as he attempted recognition.

"We can help you. Whatever it is you want we can give you."

Drew tried to respond, but his mind was mush. He had no control anymore. All he recognized were Peccadillo's fingernails scraping across his chest.

"I have been trying to warn you that the Psychic Operations are evil. They want to own you. Use you. They are only expanding your abilities to suit their needs." She turned to face the boy. Just three small steps and she was within an arm's length of Drew.

She reached out and placed both her palms on his face. He suddenly saw through her eyes. He could see himself sitting on the log, a pathetic young boy frightened by two women who wanted nothing but to help him. She let go of his head as Peccadillo turned him into her for a long exciting kiss.

Both of the girls backed away from him as he sat reeling from the attention.

Sin spoke up, "Do you know how to block your thoughts?"

"Umm. Yeah. I have done it a few times." Drew said as he regained his mental stability.

"Let me watch you." Sin said as she closed her eyes to peer into Drew's mind.

He began the ritual he had been taught, but was interrupted as he envisioned a swarm of odd looking animals looking for him.

Sin soothingly led him in a new direction. "Don't worry about the animals. That will not help you. You need to picture military men, soldiers, something that reminds you of the military."

Drew did as he was told imagining a group of the cloned drill sergeants wandering about looking for Drew. He finished the spell opening his eyes to see a huge smile plastered across Sin's face.

"Good, now let us go have some fun." Sin immediately turned toward the car and Peccadillo followed suit, grabbing the waistband of Drew's jeans as she headed out.

They piled back into the car and Peccadillo drove off

without a word. They casually drove through the town and Drew watched as the familiar sights took on a new look. Everything was so open and free, but dark. It was as if a new world had opened up to him in the twilight of the day.

He looked over at Sin feeling his thoughts unclutter. He tried to look for her psi again, but was bombarded by confused senses. He could smell her laughter tickling his nostrils. Her voice rumbled across his entire body. It was too much for him to take in. He turned his head to put her out of his view, seeing the back of Peccadillo's head.

There was an odd shadow dancing around the edges of her skin. He was mesmerized by the fluid motions of the tendrils in the darkness. They reached out to him and mingled with his own shadow. They were not shade from the sun but more of a shadow of their souls. Everything blurred and he sank into the bench seat in the back of the car. There was nothing left in him.

They arrived at the mall. The trio exited the vehicle and walked toward the entrance. It was a place Drew had been a thousand times, but for some reason it felt different that day.

There was a sense of foreboding that he could not shake. Every step he made twisted his insides, building apprehension as he neared the doors.

When the doors opened and the cool air blasted the boy, he felt shame wash over him that stuck to him like honey. The sickening thoughts of himself licked his arms and legs as they dripped to the floor.

The girls each grabbed one of his hands pulling him out of his self-deprecating daydream. They increased their speed to a slow jog pulling him through the empty aisles of the massive building. They went into an area that was nothing but closed up shops. It was an area that Drew assumed had been closed off to the public years ago.

The girls found a bench and dragged the boy down next to them. Peccadillo immediately began caressing the boy's neck and kissing his shoulders while Sin spoke in a tone that Drew could not focus on.

"Now, we can really play around." Sin let a vicious smile cross her face with a black shimmer in her eyes. The white base of her makeup clumped into revolting chunks from the sweat she had endured during the car ride. "I am going to show you how to get whatever you need."

Drew's mind was suddenly cluttered with visions of psychic instructions. He understood how to target someone's mind and alter it for his purposes. He could sense the essence of all the people inside the mall at that moment and knew with a quick thought he could have them all dancing for him.

Without a good grasp of his own thoughts, he instinctively laughed at the possibilities, seeing people forking over their cash to him, doing embarrassing dances and thanking him for doing them.

Sin filled his head with her serene voice. "Now, let's have some fun."

The girls grabbed Drew by the hands and dragged him into the mall. They ran down the walkway with no concern for others. They laughed as they nearly collided with the few patrons of the mall and fled the scene immediately upon overturning a kiosk they accidently collided with.

They ended up in the food court where Drew approached a counter. He looked into the worker's eyes peering into his personality. He could feel the boy's presence as he sent thoughts into the cashier's brain.

"Give me ten burgers, three sodas, and six sides of fries." Drew said in a measured tone still locking eyes with the boy.

The boy pressed the buttons on his register still locked into Drew's gaze. "Sixty-three, forty-two."

Drew sent an undying string of thoughts to convince the boy he was receiving a hundred dollar bill while he pulled out and handed the cashier a one. The boy took the money and gave Drew change for a hundred leaving Drew giddy with excitement.

He got his food and returned to the girls who were waiting for him at a table in the food court.

Sin let out a maniacal laugh. "I told you it would work." She grabbed a burger and began to eat.

Drew and Peccadillo joined her, cramming food down their throats. Drew ate three burgers before he felt his stomach revolt. The temperature of the mall seemed to skyrocket as he forced in a serving of French fries. And when he could consume no more he laid back on the bench refusing to move. It was that position that he remained for the next hour. He did not think, he did not move, just laid back waiting for time to pass. His relaxation was broken when Peccadillo launched a handful of fries into his face.

He shot to a sitting position and with vengeance in mind he launched a handful fries back. The three ran through the mall leaving a trail of fast food in their wake.

They eventually ended their journey in the same store the girls had taken Major Wallace. Drew stood inside the store unable to focus on any thoughts. His mind was a blur of confusion jumping from one childish thought to another.

He absent mindedly rummaged through the racks of underwear when the dressing room door opened to reveal Peccadillo wearing a bikini she was trying on from the store. A stupid grin emerged on his face.

He could do nothing but want the girl. He wanted her as an object, as a trophy, as something he had never been able to have before he met Sin. He took a couple of steps to meet the girl in the dressing room and embrace in truly lust laden kiss.

Sin stood back watching the two connect with one another. "I told you. You can have anything you want. Just stick with us, where you are free from bondage."

TWENTY THREE

THE JUNE BUG IS WHERE IT COMES FROM

Lunch time had just passed. The trio was still at the mall, now in Peccadillo's car enjoying the warmth of the afternoon. Drew lay with his head on Peccadillo's lap, his feet propped up on the back seat window. There was a stench of sweat mixed with humiliation that lingered in the car. The stink was so stingingly pungent it nearly crossed into other senses.

Drew did not understand his emotions. He expected to feel closeness with Peccadillo after their kiss. He expected a type of security with the girl's presence, but he did not. He was surrounded by a loneliness he would never have predicted.

He did not view her as the perfect person, or even someone he cared to impress. His only thoughts of the girl were demeaning opinions since she was so quick to seduce him. He did not even know her. Major Wallace barely had any memories of her and he himself had met her hours before.

Sin, seated in the front passenger seat, looked back at

the amorous couple and chuckled to herself. It was humorous for her since she had nearly all the input into their decisions. She reveled in the idea that she was more responsible than they knew for their actions.

"So, what do you think? You having fun?" Sin was poking the playful lines at Drew with the knowledge of what he would say. She could see his responses forming in his mind, but she needed him to feel that he was controlling the conversation.

"It has been great." Drew shot a smile to Peccadillo as he spoke. "But, you know my predicament." He did not want to mention his military obligations out loud. Maybe Major Wallace could get through the blocker he put up. Maybe the girls hadn't really been in his mind. Whatever it was, he was still frightened to admit anything out loud.

"I know. But we can work it out." Sin let the idea drift in and out of Drew's mind as she pulled out a vape pen. "I mean, you have a mission and if certain things are compromised, then you may be removed from your post." She puffed her addiction, filling the car with the thick scent of strawberry shortcake, covering up the lingering smells teenage sweat.

"What do you mean?" Drew was careful to not make any suggestions. His thoughts were beginning to clarify, but he refused to assume the past few hours were anything but pure freedom.

"Fine, I'll come out and say it." Sin took a deep breath as if she was going to upset someone with her words. "You need out of the military." Sin looked around to be sure the world remained silent. "That is very doable, but you have to appear to be following orders to do so unless you want a dishonorable discharge." She put in the last bit as a joke, but Drew considered it. "There are certain things the army doesn't want you to know that will get you discharged. There are actions you can take that will get you discharged. As long as they believe you are doing these things of your own free will." The last word of Sin's sentence trailed off into nothingness as if she realized what she was saying as she finished saying it.

Drew caught her mention of free will and it immediately brought thoughts into his mind about the past few hours. Had he really been doing all those activities under his own volition? His mind began to race with conspiracies when Sin shot a look at Peccadillo.

Peccadillo's hand began to trace around Drew's chest again. She pulled him up to a sitting position to plant another kiss on his lips.

Drew lost his train of thought and focused on the anxious nerve jitters he received from the affection. He drifted away from his distrust became a simple weakling.

Sin turned back to the front of the car and spouted the plan to the two in the back. "Drew, you will apprehend the both of us." Sin let the tone of her voice fall deep and monotone. "You will teleport all three of us back to the base. After your debriefing and interrogation by the military, you will be put back into the boot camp population. Be wary of what is going on because that is the point where you will have to make a choice. When the time comes you will join Peccadillo and I or you will be giving your life to the military." There was a type of threat in her voice undetected by Drew who was absorbing her words subconsciously as he held his female companion.

Sin looked for understanding in Drew's mind seeing a slight worry manifest in the depths. She responded aloud, "Don't worry about us. We have a way out." She ended it with a sinister smile to the public of the parking lot and in a momentary flash she turned the whites of her eyes pitch black.

TWENTY FOUR

FROM THE SHORE OF YOUR

The barrack seemed barren after having spent a handful of hours back at home. It was still lights out when Drew returned to the base with the two girls in tow. Major Wallace went with him to turn the girls in for questioning, getting both Drew and himself a couple of metaphoric pats on the back for a job well done.

He waited, staring at the steel ceiling, and hoping that what Sin had said was correct. Hopefully, he could be out of the military within hours.

The door opened slowly in an obvious attempt not to wake the occupants of the room even though neither Sam nor Drew were asleep.

Drew looked over at the slight squeak of the door and saw Major Wallace back to his original form quietly entering the room. He headed straight for Drew's bunk tapping him on the foot to get his attention.

Drew sat upright trying to remember his army etiquette.

"Private, you need to come with me to get debriefed and inspected for damage." Major Wallace stated what he needed with the courtesy of near silence for Sam's sake.

Drew did as he was told shuddering slightly from the reference to him as equipment. Shouldn't he be inspected for injuries not damage? He brushed the slight insult off and got dressed. The habit to shave and shower had become so routine that he completed the entire ritual within minutes of Major Wallace's request.

Wallace escorted Drew through the camp passing by the gates of Hell on the way. The small building in the center of the camp had a different ambience than usual. It felt almost as if something inside was hungry. He was nervous walking near it.

Once the two reached the General's office Major Wallace gave his farewell and teleported back to Drew's hometown. The school day was ending and there needed to be a Drew present in order for everything to flow properly.

Drew was left in a small office with a lack of decoration. The walls were off-white with a boring brown trim. There was a desk in the center of the office with a nice leather chair behind it. On the other side of the desk Drew sat in a bronze folding chair. There was no nobility in the office. It was the work place of a man who knew he was not God. The single window to the side of the desk looked out upon the building Cerberus was guarding. The invisible dog still gave Drew internal chills.

The door behind Drew opened and he came to

attention. The general walked in with more stature than Drew thought humanly possible. He was humongous, towering over the boy as if he was more statue than mammal.

General Pounder looked at the boy, involuntarily flexing his huge muscles causing the veins to protrude the smallest bit. "You are possessed." He let this statement fall with such casualness that it shocked Drew. He did not expect such normality from someone so high up on the chain of command.

The gargantuan man placed his hands on Drew's shoulders nearly engulfing the upper quarter of the boy's body. His gravelly voice boomed throughout the room, "Hold still, kid."

There was a tremendous pressure upon his shoulders as if something was trying to crush his bones, but the man was barely touching him. Drew took a deep breath while General Pounder lifted his arms into the air while simultaneously relieving the weight from Drew.

Drew could think clearly now. He was no longer worried about getting out of the army or whether or not they were evil. It all just floated away.

The general sat down in the big leather chair across from Drew. "Feel better, soldier?" The man had a smirk on his face.

"Yes, sir. I do, sir." Drew was in awe of his newfound comfort.

"It appears the enemy targeted you at some point, and you have been slowly possessed by an evil force. It was simple enough to lift, but you are obviously facing a threat beyond your ability." The general paused to think. "After the debriefing I will run down some protections you can use. So, tell me what you can about this Sin person." He looked over to Drew expecting a response, but instead the entire building shook.

There was a terrible cracking sound coming from above, echoing throughout the base. The buildings shook, rattling the steel construction. Dust and dirt fell into Drew's face as he followed General Pounder's lead of rushing to the window. As he got there a deafening boom visually bowed the window slightly.

Looking out into the base, there was a bright light shining out across the ground. It was coming from the building that Cerberus had been guarding. It was split open like a dropped watermelon, spewing flames into the sky lighting the inside of the mountain allowing the soldiers to see the rocky roof of their educational prison.

General Pounder muttered to himself, "They got Cerberus."

Drew looked at the General, confused by the situation.

"Come on, soldier. We are under attack! Forget the debriefing - get out there and fight!" He shoved Drew with a mighty force that launched him half way to the door.

The world took on a surreal feel all of a sudden. Each step shook his vision as if his eyes were a camcorder wobbling from the impact. He pushed open the door to walk out into the base. The flames towering out of the small building to the side burned his cheek. In front of him was the brig which had also been cracked open and had embers burning at the split.

There was shouting all around as the recruits used various methods of psychic force to attack the beings flying overhead. He could see psi being thrown with poisonous intentions, people launching items telekinetically, and bodies left empty as their owners flew out of them to fight in spirit form.

Drew did not know where to go or what to do. He looked up into the air to see Peccadillo and Sin flying together, hands adjoined as they motioned toward pieces of rock above them, psychically forcing them to fall toward the soldiers below. Sin let out a laugh that drowned out all the fire, crashing, and screaming.

She stopped in midair shooting psi from her palms that encased a couple of soldier's spirits. They were the grey haired drill sergeant and the blond haired female recruit. They seemed to be locked inside the psi cube unable to return to their bodies.

Drew could see the panic on their face as a short squatty man flew up to the cube. He was rather orange in color and he was in the most fit condition Drew had ever seen in a person. It only took a second for Drew to recognize the man as one of the inspirational posters at HappyLand. In the poster he was signing a last will and testament. Drew was shocked at the connection, but he couldn't make any sense of it.

The orange man sneered at the two bodiless souls forcing them both into calamity. They flung their spirits against the sides of the cube in an attempt to free themselves, but before they could the orange man expelled fire from his mouth as if it were a vast stream of flaming vomit. The trail of flames went directly to the soulless bodies of the two soldiers below burning their nonresponsive flesh leaving a thick scent. It forced bile into Drew's mouth as he saw two human being's skin melt in the heat of the attack.

As their bones charred from blood red to a vile black, the silver cords that tethered the bodies to their souls faded away as did the spirits of the drill sergeant and his psi connected female private.

Drew had a sudden realization watching the death of two people he knew, although he did not care for them, that he was currently on the side of good and Sin was not. He looked up at the girls flying in circles reveling in their destruction of human being's lives.

Sin spoke psychically to him, "This is it, Drew. You are either with us or against us. I'll see you at school with your decision." She squeezed Peccadillo's hand causing the girl to let out a lustful hiss directed at Drew.

At that moment the girls and the orange man flew out into the darkness away from camp and disappeared leaving a disaster area below. Drew looked around to see buildings destroyed, soldiers killed, and an undying flame erupting from the building housing the gates of Hell.

General Pounder walked up to Drew with a grim look

of sorrow on his face. "You alright, soldier?" It was customary more than anything else.

"Yes, but what happened?"

"When we were interrogating Peccadillo before we attempted to remove her possession, Sarah broke free. She grabbed Peccadillo and broke Lucky out of the underworld." He looked down in disgust of his lack of commanding skills for the situation.

"Underworld?" Drew was confused again.

"That building over there, with the fire coming out the top. That is the entrance to Hell, we had confined Lucky there for the last hundred years or so, but now he is out again."

Everything was beyond belief all of a sudden. How could the good guys condemn someone to Hell? How could that someone be alive after one hundred years? And who was Lucky? Drew posed the last of the questions to the General.

"Sir? If I may, who is Lucky?"

"Right, we haven't told you. Lucky is kind of immortal."

TWENTY FIVE

SEPTEMBER IS A FINE TIME FOR A BALCONY

Drew sat alone in his barracks going over what he learned during his debriefing. He had not expected to be gaining knowledge while he was spewing what had happened to him.

Soon he would be informed that he was cleared to teleport back to school. Once there he was to find Wallace and apprehend the girls. It seemed too much to ask of him. As a recruit he still knew very little of his abilities, and he had failed in capturing them once. He needed to calm himself, there were no other options, and he had his orders.

He sat on his bunk running the words General Pounder spoke to him over in his head. "Peccadillo is possessed so try not to harm her. Sin sold her soul to Lucky, be careful of her." His stomach was tied in knots. He was too uneasy to completely relax.

He had his possession fully removed, and he had a new blocker up that should keep Sin out of his mind, but he still felt like he was walking into a suicide mission. He had watched the girl jovially murder people at Fort Inspire. The image of the grey-haired drill sergeant and the blond-haired girl watching their own deaths stained his psyche with the evil that he was about to face.

The door cracked open. "You are clear to head out, soldier." The clone-ish drill sergeant closed the door leaving Drew to prepare for his trip.

Drew closed his eyes and envisioned the bathroom at the school. He could see the blue tile, shiny from a recent wash down by the janitor. Pulling out of his vision from there, he saw the pattern of tiles spread to create an entire floor. Then the stalls and urinals and sinks and door… As the sharp scent of cleaning liquid hit his brain, he opened his eyes to reveal that he was indeed inside the restroom.

So many hours had passed, it was nearly midnight. Major Wallace should be at his house asleep, but Drew knew better. There was nothing more important than defeating Lucky.

He emerged from the bathroom to enter the hallway of the school. It was dark, the lights were out for the night. He looked around thinking there might be someone there to catch him, but he was completely alone.

As he shuffled down the hallway he questioned his choice of location. Why had he gone back to the school? He understood the process of teleportation so why didn't he go home? It was all very curious to him.

He felt around the hallway with his hands gliding across cool steel lockers with the occasional break of a fire proof wooden door. The carpet scraped under his boots and he swayed his head about as if he was fending something off with his face.

When he turned the corner, he could see some light coming in from a doorway giving him a target to move toward. His pace rose as he darted for the exit.

He reached the door, but the push bar would not budge the door. It was locked. He peered outside to see if anyone would be there to hear him break through the glass, but someone was there.

Sin and Peccadillo were in the parking lot, both glowing a dark red. They appeared to be chanting something with Major Wallace adorned as Drew kneeling between the girls. He kept trying to stand, but each time the girls would grab him by the arm and he melted back to the pavement.

Drew hoped his blocker would keep Sin out of his head as he steadied his face to not give anything away to the girls. He looked out stone faced as the girls laughed mercilessly at the Major as he crumbled to pieces time and time again.

Peccadillo turned and noticed Drew standing helpless inside the locked school. She brought it to Sin's attention.

Sin turned to face Drew trying to force her mind inside his, but she could not get in. She screamed out into the world so Drew could hear her, "A worthy foe or a magnificent ally. Let's see, shall we?"

As her words faded off into the neighborhood around them the push bar clicked forward on the door releasing the lock. Drew moved forward opening the door to the outside and acknowledging Sin for releasing him from his prison. He walked out into the parking lot keeping his eyes locked on Sin's. He spent most of his energy keeping his poker face from turning into a mask of fear.

"So, you are blocking your thoughts from me now?" Sin said in a playful voice. "Well let's see your allegiance." She stepped back from Major Wallace as did Peccadillo, leaving Drew fifty feet of freedom from the two women.

Drew took a deep breath and raised his hands pointing his palms at Major Wallace. He felt the rumble within his gut as he created a purpose for the psi he was about to expel. Major Wallace, in Drew's own face, looked up at the boy looking for pity.

He scanned Drew's thoughts to find out that Drew was not about to assassinate him. He gave it away as Peccadillo saw the relief stream through Major Wallace and the girls charged.

Drew, with only seconds to act, released the psi creating a protective bubble around Major Wallace and himself. It formed just in time as the girls both bounced off the cube and fell to their knees.

Sin was furious. She let out a shriek that caused Drew to claw at his ears. Her eyes lost all color becoming black orbs in her head. Her hair began to flow as if the strands were slender snakes slithering away her scalp and a blood red aura emitted from her skin that was visible with the naked eye,

Major Wallace stood up inside the small cube. "Nice

thinking, but we need another plan. She will break through this thing shortly."

Drew watched Sin as she transformed into the pure evil demon she truly was. "You can't call for backup?" Drew pushed on the walls, testing the stability of the cube. "That was my real plan."

"It would take them too long to mobilize. We'd be dead." Major Wallace flinched as Sin splattered a large amount of poisonous psi against the cube. He relaxed a bit as the cube bent, but remained intact.

Drew rummaged through his recent lessons trying to find a way out of the cube, stay alive, and apprehend the girls. He had thought up the cube because of the image of the blond-haired girl's death replaying in his mind, but he had not developed a full plan.

He glanced at Sin seeing knives of psi pouring from her blackened eyes and bouncing off his protective prison. Nervous, he peeked over his shoulder at Peccadillo who also seemed to be at a loss. She just stood there confused as the shadowy demons danced in her aura. It gave Drew an idea.

Drew slugged Major Wallace in the arm, "Follow my lead." He closed his eyes, forced his soul out of his physical body leaving a collapsed Drew on the floor of the cube. He waited. In between blasts from Sin's psi, he made an opening in the cube flying through it to freedom and patching the breach as he exited.

Sin laughed at a volume that would rival thunder, "Good, you can watch me kill you from afar. Enjoy the show." She continued to blast the cube with her psi, creating small stress fractures in the structure.

Drew swooped overhead taking aim at Peccadillo. He was a couple hundred feet up in the air and went into a dive-bomb toward the gangly girl.

Sin caught sight of him. "I can kill you in that form as well." She shot a glob of red psi toward his spirit forcing him off track. His momentum carried him straight into the ground, in his non-form he faded into the pavement as if he just disappeared.

Sin let out another detonation of psi onto the cube which was on the verge of shattering. "Prepare to see the hereafter." She said as she gathered an enormous amount of psi.

Drew flew back up out of the ground and straight into Peccadillo's body. The girl opened her eyes as wide as they could and she gasped for air displaying her mangled teeth. Her head tilted to the side. She focused and charged at Sin. Drew had successfully possessed Peccadillo and forced out the demon that had been in her.

Sin backhanded the approaching girl with a force that sent her flying forty feet to the side. "You think possessing her will stop me? I will kill you wherever you want. Now observe as I end your life." She leaned back releasing the tremendous psi ball.

The cube shattered sending psi shrapnel everywhere. Just as the cube dispersed, Wallace crumbled to the ground forcing his spirit out of his body and moving at light speed toward Sin. His soul crashed into the demonic girl forcing her backward, falling to her back with her head bouncing off the pavement.

Drew saw Major Wallace's maneuver and could feel Peccadillo's confusion in the body he currently inhabited. He decided now was the only shot he had. Drew ejected his spirit from the girl's body and back to his own. Peccadillo stood still trying to regain her bearings as Drew's body seemed to rise from the dead.

He built the psi as quickly as he could while watching Major Wallace fly from Sin's body back to his own. Sin was unconscious lying perfectly still on the asphalt as a dark red pool of blood gathered at the back of her skull.

Wallace rose to his feet and let out a stream of psi at the same time as Drew. Drew's psi created an imprisoning cube around Peccadillo while Wallace's created one around the injured Sin.

Major Wallace used telepathy to contact base. He informed them the girls were under lock and key.

Drew looked at Sin as the blood mingled with her black clothes creating the appearance she would never wake up.

He looked at Peccadillo. The girl was physically unhurt, but her life had been destroyed. Drew did not know how long she had been possessed, but it would be hard to recover. She had been a drunken spectator to her own life, unable to make any decisions of her own. She had committed atrocities against her morals, her personality, and her fellow man.

She knelt inside the cube and sobbed into her hands. She was not just violated, she was destroyed. She had been forced to kill people, to run away from her family, and seduce a stranger. But the worst thing was, no matter how much it violated her values, her memories were of her enjoying it. She remembered being evil and now it had assassinated her self-worth.

After a couple of minutes of watching Peccadillo, Drew noticed that her movements stopped. Her tears no longer flowed, nor did the wind blow. Time had stopped.

TWENTY SIX

WHAT AM I MISSING

The air had an odd staleness with time stopped. Drew swallowed as he looked back at Sin expecting to see her standing up controlling time. To his relief she was still lying in her blood. The image caused Drew to shake physically. The reality of the danger finally hit home.

"ATTENION!" A husky voice came from behind Drew nearly startling him out of his body.

He turned to face the voice trying to revert to his military habits. He was greeted by General Pounder and two soldiers at his side carrying large glowing guns.

"Good job, soldiers. These two will be taken back to base and reviewed for imprisonment or rehabilitation." General Pounder seemed to be more upbeat than Drew had ever seen him.

Major Wallace spoke up. "Sir, the one known as Sin should be put in psychic bondage so she doesn't break out again."

"I've already got it taken care of, Major." General

turned to Drew allowing his face to grow serious. "We need to recapture Lucky. But he has barricaded himself into one of his hiding places. We cannot get in to apprehend him, so we need to send in someone who was invited." He paused, waiting for the realization to hit Drew, but it did not happen. "That is you, Private. He and his minion, Sin, have invited you into his army. You have to go in and get him out so we can grab him." The horrifying thought crawled across Drew's face. "Major Wallace will brief you on what you need to know. Again, good work, men."

General Pounder turned on his heel to confer with the two gun-toting soldiers.

Drew felt the breath shoot out of his lungs. His mind had suddenly become convinced that he was doomed to an eternity in Hell. How could he possibly face Lucky alone?

Major Wallace saw the terror in the boy's eyes and put a hand on his shoulder to try to calm him. "It isn't going to be like what you're thinking."

Drew was astonished at the gall of the Major to try to and tell him that facing the fallen angel, the embodiment of evil, would not be that bad. He tried to respond, he tried to make a defiant noise, but nothing came out.

"You only need to convince him to come out and an entire platoon will take him on. You won't be fighting hand to hand with him or anything like that." Major Wallace realized that this was not putting Drew at ease. "He has no interest in hurting you personally. He was responsible for the debauchery of Rome, every war humanity has ever waged, the holocaust… If he can't condemn millions of lives, it won't be worth it to him. So, you see, he isn't trying to send you to Hell. He wants you as a minion, just like Sin. Now that he is out of bondage, he has a plan for what he wants to do. He just needs minions to help him do it."

Drew took a breath, staring at the ground. "What do I have to do?"

"It is really pretty simple. Convince him you are under his command and that you want to help him destroy the world. But you have to be careful. He is much more powerful than you are. You are in training and he is the most powerful being ever to exist, to our knowledge. So, do not try to block your thoughts."

"But won't that give me away? Won't he see me thinking about how to get him out of his hiding place?"

"Not if you don't think it."

This was a shock to Drew. Now, not only did he have to face Lucky on his own, but he could not think what he wanted. He had to think about what he said or the mission would fail. Moreover, no matter what Major Wallace thought was safe, Drew would still be facing an enemy. There was no way he would be taking that lightly.

TWENTY SEVEN

REDDINGS OR READINGS

There was no question in Drew's or Major Wallace's mind about where Lucky was hiding. They had both been inside the mall feeling the sickening darkness within. It was not Hell, but it was the true home of Lucky.

Drew drove very slowly towards his doom. The blue hatchback crept along with the same reluctance Drew felt, as if the car read Drew's thoughts. He kept a few miles under the speed limit only to keep his own nerves settled.

The ride was nearly twice as long as it needed to be and even that did nothing for Drew's anxiety. He sat at the last light before the mall. He just sat still just staring at the huge grey building. The dull colors almost inviting him, screaming at him that nothing extreme lay inside, but he knew that to be a lie.

Drew thought he heard a car horn from behind, but it was not really there, time was stopped as was the rest of the population. He pressed his foot to the petal and crept through the intersection.

As the building grew in size on his approach, he chuckled at himself for following the traffic laws. He knew it was not a fear of getting in trouble with the law, but a fear of facing the inevitable.

He drove his car into the parking lot and found an empty spot near the back. He parked. Stepping out of the car he kept repeating a sentence to himself. "Control your thoughts, give nothing away." He stated this over and over as a mantra to keep himself out of Hell.

He repeated the mantra until he was standing just outside the automatic doors. He looked up at the dirty glass entrance. It was the perfect invitation to everything he did not want. Inside loomed a separate world, void of nature with its perfect climate and controlled lighting. It housed all the sins of man with the stores, the technology, the advertising, the rest areas… But it looked overly enticing from the heat outside the doors.

Drew took a deep breath and cleared his mind. He forced out the memories of his conversation with Major Wallace, he adjusted his memory of capturing the girls, and he erased his fears of facing Lucky.

He stepped forward causing the automatic doors to slide to the side. The gush of the air conditioned climate enveloped Drew's face. He took the steps necessary, placing himself inside the lair of Lucky.

The sense of darkness engulfed the boy just as it had the last time he came into that building. He forced his mind to cherish the darkness that seemed to radiate from the depths of the mall.

He walked down the hallway passing by frozen patrons in the midst of their shopping. He could see people with thousand dollar outfits looking at overpriced jewelry. There was an obese man sitting in the food court with four pieces of pizza in front of him. A young boy stood staring at a scantily clad woman in a poster. The entire scene was something Drew would have hated. Making the connection with evil should have made him hate the mall. However, in his current situation he reveled in the frozen people's glories. He wished he could have the money to accomplish what these people did.

His mind immediately went back to the mind control tricks Sin taught him attempting to create a plan to steal these time-stopped-people's fortune.

Drew heard a low groan coming from one of the hallways reminding him that he was there for a purpose. He was there to serve the Dark Lord or so he thought. He turned toward the groan making his way down toward the bathing suit shop where Peccadillo had kissed him.

He walked down the open hallway feeling the darkness and depression thicken around him. The air felt full and the ambience was heavy. He steadied his thoughts to a perfect stream of acceptance of the surroundings.

When he reached the end of the hallway, just past the swim suit store, he was in an open atrium. It was the staging area for a large chain store the anchor store for that end of the mall. He could see up to a second floor that surrounded the area he was now standing in. In the center of the area sat a large chair which supported Lucky.

His orange skin seemed more vivid inside the bland grey building. He looked over at Drew as the boy approached, his black eyes burning into the kid's soul. "You have a lot of nerve showing up after locking up Sin." The voice was gravelly and deep, but it seemed to come from everywhere but Lucky himself.

Drew recalled his altered memories of the confrontation. He recalled his alliance with Major Wallace as a disgusting necessity. He allowed the man to assist because he was a failure on his own. He saw Peccadillo breaking down after her possession was removed, finding pleasure in her pain, proud of taking what he did from her. Then he saw Sin as his rival. She was the only thing standing between himself and Lucky. Without her, he would be the direct report of his enemy, not the second in command.

After the thoughts manifested inside Drew's skull, he opened his mouth to verbalize, but he was cut off by Lucky.

"No need to speak, I hear you perfectly." As the words echoed throughout the mall the man smiled showing a perfect set of teeth. "Bold move, son. You are trying to fill some big shoes. Sin was quite the warrior." He leaned back on his throne of red velvet as if he was royalty. "If you want to be by my side then we will overtake humanity today, otherwise I will bide my time until I find a worthy companion to rule the Earth with me."

Drew looked up at the short man on his chair

throwing thoughts of admiration at him in furious fashion.

"Fine. Let's do it. Hand me your soul and we will conquer all." The black eyes of the fallen angel mocked Drew with his lack of comprehension.

Drew forced his thoughts into ones of joy. He told himself his day of glory was finally here, while he panicked without a thought. While he let his mind say 'Cherish this moment. This is the culmination of everything you've ever done,' he pooled psi in his belly with no particular intentions. The goo in his gut grew quickly as he told Lucky through his thoughts that he was about to give himself to evil.

He thought the words, 'I will now OBE my spirit.', but he used the last word to put intention into the psi. The moment his soul should have spewed from his third eye in an out of body experience, the psi in his belly shot out forming a clone of his ethereal body. Drew collapsed to the ground slamming his skull against the tile trying to imitate an empty body.

The psi soul floated up and drifted over toward Lucky. It was the perfect clone of Drew as it floated toward the throne of the orange man. Drew lying motionless envisioned what everything would look like from the fake spirit's point of view. He pictured Lucky from above, looking down on his high backed chair. Peering out the corner of his eye he could see Lucky's movements and imagine the other perspective as it occurred.

Lucky reached out to the clone and touched it with his middle finger. The psi turned a clear black and it shot back into Drew's body. He gasped still trying to imitate an OBE. He looked over at Lucky with confusion trying to piece together what the Lord of Darkness believed had just happened.

Words attacked Drew's ears from all angles. "I have bound your soul to me. You have given up an eternity of everlasting love for an eternity of serving me. You will have the gratification of satisfying me." He rose to his feet motioning for Drew to rise as well.

He placed his hot hands upon Drew's cheeks forcing a few lifetimes of education in natural sorcery into Drew's mind in a matter of seconds. "You defeated Sin, you must be a formidable warrior. This should put you on level ground with the 'holier than thou' army outside. Go and show them what we are capable of. Then, once you have shown me you are powerful enough and intelligent enough, I will come. I will rise from my pit and we shall conquer. I will reign again. This will be the beginning of the Age of Shadows." The world shook as his speech ceased.

Drew let butterflies take hold of his gut convincing himself they were nerves of anticipation as opposed to anxiety. He spoke to Lucky for the first time. "Yes, master." He turned on his heel and marched back toward the door of the mall. He could not question anything. Lucky would still have his mind trained on Drew's. He just took pride in the idea that he had just lost his soul. Not even able to wonder if his trick had worked or how he would find out.

As the darkness lifted as he neared the sliding doors,

Drew felt the pressure of Lucky's presence wane. He stood at the entrance just outside the reach of the door's sensors. His stomach tied in knots from the fear of the battle he was about to wage.

He took a deep breath to relax himself and then took a step. The door opened allowing entrance to Drew's new battle, his fight against the United States Army Psychic Operations.

TWENTY EIGHT

GIVE IN TO MY WILL

The doors opened to allow the cold air to eject from the mall. A couple of steps put Drew in the heat of the day. It was an odd sensation when moving farther away from evil.

Drew looked out over the frozen landscape. There were cars that seemed to be parked on the freeway, but the people inside still seemed okay, frozen in their mundane situations. Birds were in midflight, suspended high above the ground. It was like stepping into a painting.

The only difference from when Drew had entered the building was the presence of Psychic Operations. There were a couple of tanks, a few hundred men with glowing rifles, what appeared to be a missile launcher, a couple hundred men left weaponless unless you consider their minds, General Pounder, and Major Wallace. The sight was intimidating knowing what he was about to attempt.

Drew looked to each side trying to figure out the weak spot in the military's strategy, but as one person, Drew could not spot anything.

Major Wallace came jogging up to Drew, wide eyed, wondering what happened. "Did you draw him out?" He blurted out when he was within earshot.

"I control my thoughts, I give nothing away." Drew shouted at Wallace as he lifted his boot, planting it in the center of Wallace's chest. "You will face me before him!"

The impact sent the Major backward a few feet, but the message was clear, Drew would have to face the army to draw out Lucky. Major Wallace realized the dilemma Drew was facing. If he spoke of his allegiance with the USAPO then Lucky would remain hidden, but if he didn't the USAPO might kill him.

Major Wallace sprinted back toward General Pounder as the rest of the forces went into action against Drew. "General, don't fire! He is fighting for show." He shouted as waves of psi were launched over his head.

The General stood looking on at Drew. "That may be, Major. Unfortunately, standing down won't be necessary."

Major Wallace turned around to see what the General was referring to. He was presented with a view of the most amazing feat of psychic force he had ever seen. Drew had managed to stop all the psi within feet of his body and reversed its trajectory, sending the binding goo back toward its senders.

Drew was surprised himself. The information Lucky had forced into his head was all coming out naturally with almost no effort on his own part. He had stopped the barrage of psi, not by refocusing it, but by seizing the minds of each soldier on the opposing side of the battlefield. He forced them all to redirect their intention to themselves.

He watched in forced delight as the two hundred unarmed men were encased in their own psi goo. It was binding psi that forced most of the men to the ground, barely be able to breathe under the pressure. A few men collapsed instantly making Drew realize that a few of the men had worse intentions for him than the others.

He let a smile crack his face. If it was not for his eyes keeping their color, Major Wallace would have assumed Drew had crossed over to Lucky's army.

Drew created a shield as he watched the glowing riflemen take aim at him. The shield created a deep vibrating sound that was reminiscent of electricity streaming through the air. The rifles fired at Drew stopping with a faint sizzle as the glowing blue projectiles hit the shield.

Drew snorted in disgust of how his fellow soldiers were treating him, just because he had sided with Lucky. He saw Major Wallace out of the corner of his eye. The man was astonished. He could not believe what Drew was suddenly capable of.

Drew cleared his throat training his mind on the essence of the glowing rifles. He could feel the cool steel, smell the static in the air, his mind had truly identified with the weapons. He raised his arms over his head with an unprecedented swiftness forcing all of the military's guns to shoot hundreds of feet in the air. A few of the soldiers had refused to let go and were slung shot from their posts and seconds later hit concrete with a thud, leaving them in an unmoving puddle of soldier.

Those who released their guns were greeted with the descent of the guns back toward their helmets. Drew flung his arms back down just as the guns were within striking range of the soldiers who had carried them, forcing the weapons to accelerate. Many of the Psi Guard soldiers were knocked unconscious by the falling steel.

Drew looked out at the few who still remained standing, most of them running for cover of some kind. He flung his arms wildly to each side, grabbing a different soldier with each motion psychically throwing them across the parking lot.

Drew looked at General Pounder who seemed to be lost in deep thought. He had not sent out for another attack. The tanks and missile launcher were completely still. He looked to the General's side to see an excited Major Wallace looking toward the entrance to the mall.

Drew couldn't have the Major overlooking him. He shoved the shield to the side and sprinted directly at Wallace. By the time he had caught his prey's attention, it was too late. Drew body tackled Major Wallace causing them both to land hard on the asphalt, scraping across the tiny rocks for a dozen feet. Blood immediately poured from both men's wounds.

The General was caught off guard by this move and turned his attention to get in on the action, but Drew beat him to it. He put up a physical psi barrier, keeping everyone out, but him and Major Wallace. Now the two men found themselves in the same situation they had been in outside the school earlier.

The two men were the only ones inside the cube, completely cut off from the outside world. Major Wallace relaxed feeling safe with Drew there, but Drew attacked. He OBE'd from his body and latched onto the Major's. Unlike before where he was possessing people, Drew reached in and ripped out Major Wallace's spirit.

Both of the men's bodies were lifeless on the ground as their souls grappled within the psi cube. A rumble shook the existence of Drew. "Do it." It was Lucky demanding Drew to finish off his friend.

He materialized a psi dagger and slashed at Major Wallace's silver strand in an attempt to sever his soul from his body for all eternity.

Major Wallace finally woke up. Realizing that he could not trust Drew any longer he slipped through the boy's grip and yanked his silver cord thrusting his spirit back into his body.

Drew did the same and the two men began to brawl, fist to fist. Bones cracked in Drew's shoulder under the pressure of Wallace's boot. Drew retaliated with a chop to the throat that left Wallace unable to inhale for a few seconds.

Before the two men could annihilate each other, the sky went black. All light became florescent and the air turned to a painful temperature below zero. Both men turned back to see Lucky standing in front of the mall. He was no longer a short orange man, but now a giant man adorning the skin of a dog's head on his own spewing fire from his nostrils.

The world began to shake violently causing cracks in the pavement around the building. Lucky's voice rang out across the nation, "Let us bring about the end of mankind. The world shall now suffer as I have suffered."

TWENTY NINE

JULY IS TIME TO TEACH

Drew and Major Wallace were shocked. Neither could manage to move in the presence of such a massive evil force. They both lay immobile as Lucky stepped toward General Pounder.

The missile launcher and tanks opened fire on the monstrous demon. They were no match as Lucky charged some psi to rebound the projectiles back toward the launcher. Within seconds the entire platoon was eradicated.

The General sneered as he looked up at the evil towering thirty stories over the man's head. The humongous beast snorted. The world quaked as Lucky's voice crumbled the pavement again. "Forgo the act, let us end this now!"

The General nodded and looked to the ground. His body bubbled as if he was being boiled in oil. His muscles grew in pulses as his stature rose up above the earth and he stood face to face with Lucky. His voice came out soft and quiet, yet something definitely to be feared.

Lucky reached back and thrust his fist into the face of

the giant general. As his hand crushed into the face of Pounder, Lucky disappeared. It was as if he had pressed a button and vanished.

General Pounder shook his head to regain his balance. He looked around for Lucky, but found nothing. "Come out and face me, coward."

General Pounder was hit from behind by the invisible demon taking him to his knees, toppling trees in the process. He quickly rose back to his upright position sweeping his glance across the horizon to look for his foe. "You haven't faced me in two hundred years and all you can do is hit me from behind and hide? I can't wait to send you back to the underworld."

Something hit the General's leg bending his knee slightly to the side, but it was a reference point for the military man. He reached out with his fist in the direction of the attack, catching Lucky off guard.

The villain was knocked to the ground giving away his location by crushing a car in the process of landing.

The general was quick to pursue, leaping toward the spot and pounding the ground with his fists hoping to catch his target still lying down.

Drew broke his daze from watching the two titans battle. He did not want Lucky to return to the mall if things got too intense. He quickly built some psi to barricade the mall from Lucky's return.

The second the psi left Drew, Lucky knew he had been double crossed. The cube Drew and Major Wallace were inside shattered as Lucky smashed it with a simple thought. He took off the dog skin face causing him to reappear long enough to show Drew his fate. He raised his fist in the air and brought it down with awe inspiring force. An instant before Drew was crushed to dust, General Pounder grabbed Lucky by the throat, yanking him backward and saving Drew.

Drew suddenly felt all the information Lucky had forced into him, drain out. He was left with what he had learned in boot camp and from Sin. He turned to Major Wallace who was a puddle of lifelessness. Drew got the hint and projected his spirit outside of his body.

The two soldiers flew through the air launching psi on Lucky so if he became invisible again they could track him from the psi splatters.

The General thrust his palm into Lucky's chest sending him flying backward hundreds of yards. Hitting the ground, he piled up lips of destruction as he slid. Lucky grabbed the debris and launched it at the General. It caught Pounder on the side of the head taking him down for a moment.

Lucky turned to the two annoying souls zipping by his head. They were no threat, but an unkindly nuisance. He shot a glob of psi just narrowly missing Drew.

Major Wallace screamed at Drew, "Don't let him hit you. That psi is charged to kill your soul, not just your body."

This information was enough to send Drew away from the action.

The two behemoths continued to tear into each other

leaving destroyed buildings in their path. Lightning began to come down from the sky each time either of the men struck a blow and Drew stopped trying to remember the information that Lucky had ripped away from him.

He had no recollection, but he felt an idea brew.

He looked at the General who was downed from a powerful blow from Lucky. On the other side he could see Major Wallace getting to his feet, having retreated from his spiritual attack on Lucky.

Drew turned his attention back toward the enemy in time to see a large ball of death psi heading straight toward him.

THIRTY

IS IT ME OR IS IT YOU

Drew tried to build psi the second he saw the attack coming, but it was too late. The death psi sunk into the soul of Drew flying high above his body.

Lucky let out a laugh as his target vanquished.

Drew's spirit fell from the sky tumbling head over heels as he careened to the Earth. As he fell, he began to glow a cool blue. The descent slowed and a large ball of psi expelled itself from his body. The psi shot at Lucky, and Drew's spirit went in the opposite direction.

The psi sank into Lucky and bound him to the ground, completely unable to move. General Pounder got to his feet as he shrank back down to normal size. He made his way over to Lucky. He slapped some psi around Lucky's wrists to officially apprehend him.

Major Wallace watched Drew spiral across the sky, assuming he had sacrificed his life for humanity. He saluted the soul as it crashed deep into the ground.

He looked at Drew's body ready, to lift it up and

teleport him to base. He walked over with a tear in his eye for his fallen friend when he noticed the silver chord still attached to the body. He reached down and yanked the strand forcing Drew's soul back into his body.

Drew was becoming more accustomed to getting shot back into his body and simply opened his eyes to see Wallace staring down at him in disbelief.

"How?" Said Major Wallace forgetting his military etiquette.

Drew laughed at the demand arriving so quickly after he nearly died. "As soon as I saw his shot, I knew I couldn't avoid getting hit." He coughed, his body not used to so much abuse, nor was his spirit. "But, as it got to me I realized I could recharge it before it affected me. So, I took the hit trying to recharge it to a binding psi before it latched onto my ethereal body. Then I shot it back at him." He paused again. "Did it work?"

Major Wallace chuckled. "It worked. Now you will most likely be promoted. You will probably get some awards and medals. You may get to meet the President. But now that you are still alive." Wallace paused for drama. "You will have to go back and finish boot camp."

Drew laid his head back in disbelief. After all that and he did not even get to take any leave.

THIRTY ONE

EPILOGUE: JUST A LITTLE BIT MORE

He loaded his tuba into the small hatchback and waved at the couple of friends he had made thanks to Major Wallace's attendance at the Band Dance the Saturday after their fight with Lucky. Although Major Wallace felt he had failed the popularity task, it was miles above where Drew had left the situation himself.

He was in a rush. His schedule started in just a few minutes. Even though it was just a cover job to explain where his military paychecks came from, he still took it seriously.

He careened around the corners of the streets leading him to the mall. He hit the light. He looked up at the red circle forcing him to wait. As soon as the green arrow appeared he was on the move. He couldn't wait to get to work.

He pulled up to the mall, parking in the back as all the employees were instructed to do. Most did not follow the rule, but ever since he got through boot camp, he felt the need to adjust to rules.

The mall was a different place after they put Lucky

back in Hell. There was no darkness that loomed over it, no ambience that led people to excessive sins, just the cold flow of the air conditioner. It still amazed Drew how efficiently the USAPO cleaned up the destruction left from the battle, all cars returned, all buildings repaired, and no one had noticed a thing.

He got out of his car and sprinted into the building. He made corners at full speed trying to get to the movie theatre. Lucky for him, he was so talented at mind reading he knew if someone was around a corner. He never collided with patrons.

He got to the theatre and waved at Peccadillo. She had been put into rehab and eventually recruited into the USAPO. Now, they not only served together, but worked their cover jobs together as well.

Drew jumped the stairs, taking two or three steps at a time to get to the projector room. He only had a couple of minutes before he had to reel a film. He reached the top of the stairs just in time.

He barely reeled the film in time for its four o'clock showing. He collapsed into the chair next to the projector. He had forty-five minutes before he had to reel another one. He kicked his feet up and watched the comedy as it rolled through the opening credits.

He wondered why Peccadillo took the concessions job. She not only had to serve in the Psychic Operations, but she had to actually work at her cover job too. Drew knew he had it easy, just watching movies all shift.

Just as he started to relax, the door to the projection room slammed against the wall. Alarm raised the hairs on Drew's arm. He turned to see who it was.

He relaxed. It was Daisy standing in the doorway in all her beauty. The light from the hallway sent her silhouette into Drew's eyes bringing up feelings of pure ecstasy in his mind.

"Did I scare ya?" Daisy said trying to sound vicious, but coming off as campy sleepover horror movie.

"I was terrified." Drew appeased his girlfriend.

After Drew came back from boot camp, Daisy told him how much it meant to her that he was sorry for what he did and that he remembered after all those years. Thanks to Major Wallace, Drew's greatest dream had come true.

Daisy sat in the chair next to Drew. He put his arm around her, feeling complete just being close to the girl. He turned to kiss her, but her eyes had glazed over.

Startled he looked at her stunned face realizing she was frozen. He jumped from his seat in terror to see General Pounder. He had teleported and frozen time.

"Sorry to disturb you Lieutenant Darby." The General spoke with respect to the boy even though he was under rank of the General. The General was actually a species that was immortal. Drew found out after the whole ordeal that the General and Lucky battled it out every few centuries for control of humanity. Seeing how Pounder won, the foreseeable future was looking good.

"Sir." Drew fell into his military rituals quickly these

days.

The General smirked at the boy, seeing he was with a girl. Even though the General had turned out to be an eternal who remained on Earth to protect humanity did not mean he did not have a soft side. He spoke again. "We have an issue in Texas. Looks like a group of terrorists are about to take over the minds of some amusement park guests. We need you down there before we have a full scale riot."

"When do I need to depart?"

"I will say I had trouble finding you. Have a good evening with her. Ship out in four hours. Major Wallace will be here ten minutes before you leave."

"Thanks, General." He saluted the man as he disintegrated into nothingness. Drew sat back down and put his arms around Daisy. She snuggled up to him as time began to move again. No matter what he went through, it was all worth it for this moment.

If you enjoyed this book or would like to support me, please consider leaving a rating or review. It really helps me out as well as those looking for something to read.

Reviews or ratings at

Amazon.com

Goodreads.com

Shepherd.com

Bn.com

Or where ever you buy or talk about books

Just look for Richard W. Kelly

FANTASY CASTING

I find it fun to pretend like my book is being turned into a movie and am running the casting. It gives me a chance to explain a little about my characters, highlight some actors I am a fan of and of course imagine my book is going to be a movie.

So here goes the fantasy casting for The Psi-Chotic Adventures of Drew Darby…

Drew -Someone who can be awkward yet lovable. Someone strong enough to be a lead…. Finn Wolfhard. Great in Stranger Things and IT. Very strong actor.

Major Wallace - He isn't in it much except as a shape shifter, so that would be Finn Wolfhard again. But, a smooth, young, but not high school aged, good looking dude… I like the pro wrestler MJF here. He is imposing and has a good presence on screen.

Daisy - This character is one of those She's All That type of characters where she needs to appear awkward, but also can be presented as gorgeous. For the younger group of actors, I think Thomasin McKenzie. Great in Jojo Rabbit but her work in Leave No Trace shows her more awkward side.

Sin - There is a specific look that I think of here that is not very common in Hollywood. Right now, I think of Nicola Coughlan. Her work in Derry Girls I feel helps me think she is a decent fit.

Peccadillo - When I think of Peccadillo, I think of someone who is thin and incredibly distinctive. I keep thinking Kate Micucci. She is 20 years older but this is fantasy casting, right?

General Pounder - I see someone like Michael Rooker here. I would think maybe a bit younger, but that strong hard breathing type guy.

A NOTE FROM THE AUTHOR

The original idea for this story was a video game rather than a novel. The idea was you were forced to get a job at 16 and you had to work at a McDonalds type restaurant. Feeling like you were captured and being brainwashed into working for a mega-corporation you would have to use Metal Gear type stealth tactics to escape.

That idea morphed into what Drew Darby became, starting with just the opening scene. It mixes young adult adventure with religion, magick, and puzzle solving. Of course, this was supposed to be a trilogy and maybe one day it will be. I have ideas for the other books, seems like about five of them, but the writing just doesn't come as naturally right now.

Drew Darby was my first attempt at writing something that I thought other people would cling to. This was near the end of the Harry Potter craze and mixed a bit with a series I loved as a kid, The Myth Series by Robert Asprin.

I had just read Stephen King's On Writing. So, I tried to use his methodology of daydreaming your story, then writing it down. This worked for about 75% of the book. But, I started to get antsy that I would forget things or leave too many loose ends. So, the last quarter of the book is back to the old outline technique that I used for Testament.

Like I said, this book was partially modelled after the Myth Series by Robert L. Asprin, the naming conventions mostly. If you are not familiar with it, they are all puns that involve the word myth. Puns like Myth Conceptions, Hit or Myth, Sweet Myth-tery of life… I always thought it was fun and I wanted to do the same with Psi.

The first book became the Psi-Chotic Adventures of Drew Darby. Although that wasn't as clever as I hoped. The second book was supposed to be called The Psi-rens of Love. I also considered A One Psi-ded affair, The Psi-cle of life, The Psi-entific Method, and The Psi-lent Killers.

Like I said, I have ideas for the other books. Maybe one day I will write them or maybe someone want to collaborate. I would love to co-author these to get them out there.

Either way, thanks for supporting me. I will keep on writing, please keep on reading.

A PREVIEW OF ANOTHER TALE

The next book in my catalogue is actually Kings of One Color. But that one is a bit more adult that Drew Darby is, so I am skipping ahead to The Cattercorns of Cloudville Arizona.

I consider this book a part of the Bizarro genre. If you haven't read anything in the genre you are missing out. They are wildly outlandish stories that could only occur in imagination. Be warned they are often more mature and contain violence, sex, and depravity. My entry, although a bit violent at times, is considerably more PG-13 than many in the genre.

This book was created during a conversation I had with my daughter in an attempt to come up with an outlandish idea to use for Bizarro. Thus, the tale was born.

PART I

Kermit sat on his living room floor counting the change he had pulled from under the couch. The lack of money made him want to cry. Three quarters, one dime, and two pennies was not quite enough to buy a taco. He took a deep breath as he looked to his water stained ceiling. With a loud exhale, he realized it was going to be another few days of Ramen noodles. Not that his physique couldn't handle a few days of limited calories. Kermit was a bit of a plumper.

Scott plainly ignored his broke roommate and continued to watch Wheel of Fortune desperately attempting to see through Kermit's head rather than acknowledge the blatant cry for attention. He squinted his eyes as if that would change the translucence of his friend's dark hair. He could see 'wal… head… the dog… head… ong… head… h'.

WAL______THE
DOG________ONG
______H

Scott bounced in his seat as he proudly stated, "Walking the dog but have the wrong bitch!"

The stupid guess pulled Kermit out of his self-wallowing stupor to turn and look at the television. A quick shake of his head flinging his overgrown hair from side to side brought him back to reality. He grabbed his change as he stood up to get out of the way of the screen. "I think it is 'walking the dog on a long leash'."

Scott was used to getting the puzzles wrong, he was terrible at any television game show. However, that puzzle should have been obvious. "Well if your big head wasn't in the way."

Kermit ignored the odd statement and instead tried to bum a ride off his financially advantaged roommate. "Any chance you are going to the grocery store any time soon?" His glasses slid down his nose just a bit giving off the feeling that even the inanimate objects around him were sulking for him.

"Don't have enough for gas?" Scott continued to watch Wheel, missing out on the pouty posture of his twenty two year old roommate and best friend. With only T's and A's on the board.

--- -A-- A--
--AT----T ----

"Big cans and flatulent buns?"

"No. I don't have enough to eat really. I need a ride so I can stock up on Ramen and maybe live until I get paid on Friday." There were many times that Kermit hated his best friend, but the times when he was down on money were probably the worst. Scott had it all together, at least for an early twenty something with a high school education. He was muscular, popular with the ladies, funny, financially stable… Not to say he did not have his issues. He had a bit of an overbite, buckteeth, and general goofy demeanor.

They had guessed n, r, and e.

RE- -A-E AN-
-RAT--R-T ----

"Ref babe and bratwurst logs?" Scott shook his at his wrong answer letting his short naturally red locks bounce above his visage.

"Any chance you headed that way?" He really hated it when Scott made him spell everything out. Couldn't he understand the shame in being broke and relying on people around you?

"I guess I can run up there in a bit, how about after the Wheel?" He was lost in his game, now with o, d, and s.

RED -A-E AND
-RAT--RST SO--

He barely realized what he was agreeing to, "Red male and bratwurst sock?"

"Thanks, I really need the help today." Kermit looked back at the screen and reached out to pat Scott on the shoulder. "It's red kale and bratwurst soup."

Scott gritted his lips and nodded as he realized Kermit had solved the puzzle.

Kermit waited patiently as his friend and roommate watched his television program. It seemed in times like this he would find himself thinking about his life and how he ended up where he is. Just four years before he felt like he had the world at his feet, having graduated from high school and already making money working in the telephone scam industry.

His parents had begged and pleaded with him to go to school, but he didn't understand the point. He was making ten thousand dollars on a bad month. Every time he convinced an old lady that he was a Nigerian prince, he brought in five grand. Every time he suckered a business executive into giving him access to his computer, he would make eight thousand. He was good at them all, auto warranty scams, charity scams, disaster relief scams, grandparent scams, grant scams, imposter scams… It was call center sales at its finest.

Kermit was making so much money that he managed to live on his own in the exact same two bedroom he currently shared with Scott. He was the top scammer in his center. He was doing so well the company wanted him to start thinking about management. Similar to the debate with parents about school he did not understand why he would start a management track. The pay was not as good as those in the trenches.

He turned down promotion after promotion because he could not get the SPIFs (Sales Performance Incentive Fund) that he got on the phones. He went into that dilapidated former Toys R Us five days a week for twenty-one months. He built his bank account up, even while splurging on his apartment, car, and random gadgets, to nearly a hundred seventy-five grand.

Lucky for him he never took the promotion as that February when he parked his Porsche around the corner from his employer he could already see the red and blues lighting up the street. Kermit knew instinctively that he needed to just keep driving and forget that he ever worked with Trust Us Inc.

Of course, his employment was unofficial. There were no records of who he was, just the hearsay of the other employees. Since he did not quite make it in that day he ended up avoiding arrest or any real responsibility for his actions over the previous couple of years.

Those who did happen to be on shift when the cops arrived were given a lovely forty-eight hour stay in the local lockup. They either received a small fine with some community service or were allowed to walk free if they named some of their managers.

The owners of the company were off in some far away land called Bangkok where they avoided any punishment from the United States law enforcement. They were hidden behind many VPNs, masked numbers, and location simulators. They were hidden in a similar fashion to the phones at call center. Without a lot of technical hacking type work, the phones appeared to be coming from a company in China that was routed through India that was masking itself to look like it was from the United States. It seemed like a lot of work to make phone calls from the US to the US, but after the raid, it made more sense.

Since the owners were out of reach of law enforcement, the managers took the beating. They were hit with fraud, deception, theft, and money laundering in the first round of charges. The eight of them ended up being sentenced to more time than most violent criminals.

After that scare Kermit tried to walk the straight and narrow. It wasn't because he was afraid of the law, but the people who took the fall. He did not know who ratted out the company, but with him walking away unscathed he was worried what other people would think.

Of course, the worldwide pandemic that kept everyone locked up in their house for six months, more for those in certain parts of the country or the world, put a damper on life in general. Kermit lived off his savings for a while, but a year later, when his bank account had dried up to under fifty thousand he started to get the picture that he had to find something else to help him.

The television snapped off ending the high pitch buzz that had engulfed the room. Scott hopped up to his feet from the couch rattled his keys as if he was taunting an infant, "Ready to go?" His red hair, buckteeth and acne that had not realized he was past his teenage years always made Scott look a bit like a caricature. If he wanted, he probably could have sued a dozen local computer repair companies for using his likeness with their animated geeky worker logos.

The two rode in Scott's ten-year-old Hyundai Santa Fe the eight blocks to get to the local grocery store. Their time spent together was typically meaningless. As usual on the ride they mumbled the words to songs on the radio together while pointing out attractive women in the cars they passed by. It was a strange connection they had that allowed them to appreciate one another's company while not having to have any semblance of adulthood.

Walking into a grocery store in Texas in the summer is like walking into a walk in freezer. Only in places where it gets well above the hundred degree mark, sometimes well above the hundred ten mark do they understand the importance of keeping the building the opposite of the temperature outside. There was so much air conditioning trying to keep that huge building under seventy degrees that the force of wind when the doors parted caused a bit of effort to enter. It is the same in the opposite side of the year. When it is twenty degrees outside they find it necessary to warm things up to nearly eighty degrees inside.

Scott grabbed a cart and drove through the aisles like an eight year old, attempting to ride the steel basket while gaining momentum with his feet. As he went down the aisles, he tossed random garbage foods into the basket. He threw in cookies, cereals, candy, gum, soda…

Kermit, paying attention to the hanging signs rather than his immature friend, finally found aisle fourteen where the international foods were. He thought to himself that calling prepackaged ramen noodles and international food was probably an insult to many people, but he would keep it to himself.

He knelt down on the ground to look at the different flavors. As he looked at the shelf, his heart sank. Ramen had risen to twenty-five cents a package. That was a twenty-five percent increase and the difference between three and four meals that week.

Kermit sat on his knees in the middle of the aisle staring at the sign and trying to convince his gut that he could take a day off from food. Scott came riding down aisle fourteen twenty minutes later with a basket half full of junk. The sight of his roommate silent and unmoving on the grocery store floor put him at an unease he did not like.

Over the last few months, he felt that Kermit was starting to lose his mind, so much, so that Scott had begun to lock his bedroom door at night. However, this seemed like the final straw, the final piece of the puzzle that would explain

Kermit's fall into insanity.

He slowly approached the boy and laid a gentle hand on his right shoulder. Kermit looked up into the eyes of his roommate and said, "I can eat beef today, chicken tomorrow, but then I only get one more. What is more filling shrimp or pork ramen?"

Scott nodded his head slowly understanding that it was a money issue and not a small one. "Why don't you put them all in the cart? I will buy the ramen. Let's get three of each flavor."

Kermit nodded his head as he got back to his feet and dropped the square packets into the shopping cart. His mind had forgotten where he was and returned to the replaying of his recent life.

After the year alone in the apartment, Kermit reached out to some old friends. Many of them would not speak with him as he had recruited them to the job that landed them in jail for a couple of days. But, Scott was a friend from way back. They knew each other from elementary school. They met in third grade when they were both new at their school in the panhandle of Texas. Scott in his infinite eight year old wisdom had just moved to Texas from New York City where he believed he was an urbanite and better than the random rednecks of the Amarillo. Kermit on the other hand had just moved to Amarillo from Arizona. He dressed and behaved like a hippy because his family was from Bisbee, which was a community that derived its value from local art and cuisine.

Kermit by no means resembled the kids Scott was

used to seeing in Manhattan, but he did not look like the average cowboy like the majority of his class so he gravitated towards the kid. Over the course of their public school education, they would be nearly inseparable. They were best of friends spending half their time at one family's house and the other half at the other. They both got their first job at the same steak restaurant. Of course, Kermit quit after a weekend while Scott continued to serve oversized steaks to fat cowboys that thought they could overeat for a free meal. They both obsessed over bad sci-fi films. They both took the same two girls to the prom, different years almost as if they just traded off. And they graduated on the same day, moving on to become adults.

From there Kermit went on to swindle people out of a ton of money while Scott built upon a series of skills that started to build a career in adventuring. It started with scuba diving, then he moved onto rock climbing, he got a pilot's license, motorcycle license, truckers license, learned how to bushwhack, navigate by the stars, and sail. He became the go to guy for any type of adventure.

Although he loved going treasure hunting, most of the time he was recruited for late night stakeouts of haunted buildings. All the physical training he had endured was typically wasted on sitting in a dark room reading an EMF meter while a group of superstitious wimps talked about chills in the air or things moving that never moved. It did not matter much as Scott was well compensated no matter what kind of adventure he was commissioned to take.

When they returned from the grocery store, Scott took on the parental role with his friend. He had Kermit lie on the couch and stare off into whatever the evening cop drama was playing on the television.

Scott prepared a bowl of Ramen noodles with a side of saltines to hopefully bring his roommate out of his stupor. "Here you go." Scott placed the food down on the coffee table in front of their couch. "Why don't you get some food in your stomach?"

Kermit nodded and turned his focus to the bowl of soup. He returned to his replaying of the last few years as he ate his food.

When Scott moved into the apartment, everything fell apart very slowly. His money dwindled. He had no skills that an upstanding company would want, so he returned to the call center world as an I.T. support person for a retail chain. This was of course after the pandemic where companies were no longer providing offices, phones, and computers. Instead, Kermit would work from his bedroom using his own phone and computer that he paid for.

The job was essentially reading a script to someone in a retail store that was having issues with their register or computer or security system. He would find their particular issue and read the script. When it did not fix their issue, he transferred them to another technical agent who had the script for the next level of urgency. He went from making ten plus thousand dollars a month to working full time and after taxes not bringing in a thousand bucks each month.

With the rent, food, insurance, and general life expenditures he continuously fell farther and farther behind until the bank account ran dry.

The first time he ran out of money Scott was away for the weekend helping someone attempt to capture a chupacabra in northern Mexico. It was the first time Kermit thought he had hit rock bottom. He would be able to go a few levels lower, but that weekend while he ate a questionable apple out of the crisper in the fridge along with an old can of beets for dinner he thought about how far he had fallen.

He enjoyed the company of Scott and of course, the money that he contributed, but over the near year, he had been there, Kermit never saw him struggle. That part put him over the edge. Kermit had crashed and burned while Scott had created this cushy and soft life himself.

The anger he felt from his roommate's success was somewhat deserved as Kermit always assumed there would be a point where he might have to take advantage of Scott to get back on his feet. Regardless of the past between the two boys, Kermit had become hardened in the scamming world and was willing to take those traits back to his real life.

Scott grabbed the bowl to return it to the kitchen. He knew that if he did not do the simple work that bowl would stay on the coffee table for weeks on end until it grew something that grossed out Kermit. Suffice it to say, Kermit was not the cleanest of people.

Scott feeling like he needed to do something to make sure his roommate and old friend was still in that lost shell of a person started a conversation, "Kermit, do you know why I always loved being your friend?"

Kermit looked up at Scott annoyed at his luck and easy life. "No. I thought it was because I wasn't a shit kicking asshole redneck."

Scott ran his hand through his curly red hair and chuckled at Kermit's blunt answer. "That is why I first talked to you. But, no. I always liked hearing your strange stories about Arizona."

This brought a smile to Kermit's face. He had not thought about Arizona in years. It was so far back that he had trouble remembering much about the place. His annoyance with Scott started to fade as he engaged in the conversation. "What the stories of the strange hippies? Or the putrid water that seemed to only come out at the restaurants?" He laughed at his few and broken memories.

"Actually, I was always enthralled with a story you told me about a treasure." Scott leaned back in his chair. Facing his pudgy distraught friend, he tried to remind him of the tale he had once told him. "I believe there was a heist of some sort."

Kermit's eyes glazed over a bit as his mind reached for the threads of memory that remained of the story. "That's right. In the late 1800s, there was a small sect of Grabull Indians that roamed the mountains of southeast Arizona. As America grew west, they watched from atop the mountains as their lands were taken and destroyed. They watched as their Indian rivals were imprisoned and killed."

Scott snapped and pointed at Kermit trying to encourage him to continue the story.

"As the colonization of America came to their mountains, they knew from watching the rest of the Indian tribes that they stood no chance against the technology and viciousness of the Americans. Rather than put up a fight they collected all of their most sacred possessions, their belts, their weapons, their herbs, their drawings of their prayers and religious stories, and most of all the one thing the colonial destroyers were after, the secret to the entrance of the gold mine. The gold was at one time the life force of the mountains they called. They put all these things into a satchel made from the skin of a cat. They gave the satchel to their shaman who pleaded to the Gods to take care of their satchel until the time came when a new generation of the Grabull tribe could take back their lands. He asked for the God of the Wind to protect all the items and all the people of their tribe with the force of the tornado. He asked for the God of the Rains to drown any man who dare to harm their tribe or steal their sacred items. He asked the God of Earth to protect the items in the satchel by raising the land to the sky where no one could access it again. And he asked the Creator God to turn the tribe into the most vicious of creatures to protect their sacred items."

Scott was at the edge of his seat now and waiting for the big ending. "Go on!"

Kermit looked up and stared straight into his roommate's eyes, "When the Americans who had already taken over most of Arizona came up the mountains where the Grabull waited a great event happened. A group of soldiers confronted the tribe with their guns aimed at the Indian tribe who nearly welcomed the invasion. The men expected a fight and when they did not get one, they started taking possessions from the tribe members. When they reached the shaman and they grabbed the satchel the heavens opened up. First, a tornado took the men and threw them into the sky. Rains poured down on them as they gasped for breath and finally the mountain itself shot up from the ground and took the tribe and soldiers into the clouds where no one would ever see them again." He paused and relished in the moment as Scott was captured by every word that Kermit said. "To this day if you find the right mountain in Arizona you will see that it rises into the clouds beyond what anyone can see. There lies the satchel, the shaman who protects that satchel and the transformed Grabull tribe protecting what's left of their society. Many have tried to find it, but none have ever returned from Cloudville, Arizona." There was more to the story. Something about a chosen one, some kind of reptile that would bring the Grabull of old and the Grabull of new back to Earth where they would return to their purpose and be a part of the cycles of nature. He always left that part out because he never could remember enough details to tell the tale.

"That's the one." Scott looked up at the ceiling as he leaned back into his chair enjoying the story that led him to his profession. "It's inspiring, isn't it?"

"The stupid Indian story?" Kermit was shocked that Scott would entertain such ridiculous ideas.

"Kermit, I am a treasure hunter. You told me that story when I was eight or nine years old. After years of research and adventuring, I know that it probably isn't a very accurate story, but it is what got me into this business in the first place. And I bet there is some truth to it."

The conversation was starting to go so far over the deep end, Kermit started to question his own sanity. The idea that some ancient shaman put some trinkets in a purse and then enticed Gods to create a cataclysm to protect it was insanity. He threw up his hands laughing at his eccentric roommate and went to his room to get a little bit of early shuteye.

But lying in bed the story kept roaming around in his head. He kept thinking back to his childhood in Arizona with the crazy hippies that believed the story. They would have séances to try to speak to the shaman, they chanted and meditated on the hills in the presence of wildflowers. And, the more he thought about it, the more he remembered driving through southeast Arizona and seeing a mountain that rose up into the clouds.

Lying in bed falling in and out of sleep he questioned why Scott wanted to hear the story. He had talked of inspiration and truth within it. As much as Kermit did not want to think about it, Scott wanted to go searching for the treasure of Cloudville, Arizona.

The idea was ridiculous. There was no treasure.

There was no Cloudville. There was nothing but a boring ride through southeast Arizona looking for nothing. Kermit had other things to worry about. Things like money. Things like former bosses that may show up at his house to teach him a lesson in snitching. But, as he pondered the ways in which he would be beaten and tortured he started to think that maybe it didn't have to happen. Maybe he had found the purpose for Scott being his roommate.

After an exhausting night of tossing, turning, worrying, and hoping Kermit emerged from his room to find Scott still in the living with a bunch of old books spread out on the floor and coffee table.

Kermit had seen this before, Scott was preparing to go on an adventure, and this was his typical ritual for preparation. "What is all this?" Kermit posed the question with as much hesitancy as humanly possible.

"I started thinking about the Cloudville treasure. If we are going to go find it, we need to have a starting place. I looked up Grabull, Arizona, Cloudville, Indian Gods, and then all the different mountain ranges in Arizona in my tenth edition of the Britannica." Scott was speaking a million words a minute.

"Stop!" Kermit shouted which was quite out of character for him. "What do you mean if we go and find the treasure? I cannot go and find a treasure. First, I have a job I have to do. Second, I have bigger issues like how to find enough money to eat. In addition, most importantly. And don't let me downplay this at all, but it doesn't exist!" The shouting returned with the end of the sentiment.

Scott was taken aback by the abrupt and loud speech, but felt that these things were not issues. "You hate your job and make shit for money. Let's look at it this way. Normally, when I go on a trip someone has commissioned me to do so. They pay me to help them accomplish their goal. I will commission you to help me. That way you don't have to worry about eating or your shitty job."

Scott kept talking, but Kermit was trying to process that he was just offered money. It was better than he expected. He had started developing a plan where he could sublet the apartment while they were gone and hopefully be the ones to meet his former managers if it must happen, but if Scott was going to pay him on top of that. It was as if his world of troubles saw a temporary relief point. He knew it was not a solution to all his issues, but it felt like the event that needed to happen to get his scamming skills back on track.

"I have found multiple mountain ranges in these books that appear to be obscured by google maps, so there may be something in one of those places. I also have found pieces of the story that you told me in the Indian Gods section of the encyclopedia, but it isn't as detailed as what you…"

Kermit, still not listening, interrupted his best friend. "How much?"

Scott stopped talking and raised a single eyebrow. "How much of what? How much detail did you provide that

I couldn't find in…"

"How much are you going to pay me to come with you?" He knew that it was poor form to ask at that exact moment, but his mind would not let him think of anything else. If he did not ask, everything Scott said would have drifted right on by.

"Oh." Scott thought for a minute. "How about this. I will cover all our bills here as well as our expenses while we are searching. That way you don't have to worry about anything."

"I have to quit my job. What do I do when we are done and I have no job?" He did not mean to ask the question, it just slipped out. His habits from his old job were kicking in. He smelt money and was pushing for all he could get. His gaze fell to his feet trying to appear ashamed for demanding support from his friend.

"We will find you another shitty job before I ask you to start picking up your half again. Plus, we will split what we find so we should be rich by the time we come back anyway." Scott had a huge grin on his face and was rubbing his hands together with excitement.

Although the conversation was what was needed to get both of the young men on board with the trip it was also what sealed their fate from ever returning to that dingy apartment. It was the adventure of a lifetime and they were both committed to seeing it through.

Excited for a break from his internal worry, Kermit spent the next few days burning through the large stash of

Ramen noodles that Scott had purchased. Without a care for money he wanted the next most important thing to him, to feel satisfied.

Scott on the other hand kept himself busy with his research. He learned as much as he could about the legend, the area, and the Grabull. His preparation was something he always prided himself in being the best in. He had made printed out aerial maps from Google and compared it to his old Atlas that gave the topographical elevation changes. He had several spots that he wanted to investigate as the elevations were excessively high, unconfirmed, or the Google images were blurred.

With Scott fully wrapped up in his trip Kermit was able to find a small family that was interested in subleasing the apartment for however long they could get it. He had both the family and Scott depositing money into his bank account which would then cover rent with the apartment complex. He could feel that his bank account was on its way back to building up.

Scott packed all his adventure gear. The Santa Fe was packed to rims with tents, hammocks, sleeping bags, extra clothes, ton of water, fire making tools, bushwhacking tools, rock climbing gear, a vast array of weaponry ready to take on whatever the mythical beasts were in the legend. His stash included bug spray, sunscreen, first aid kits, canned oxygen, and even his scuba suit although he didn't expect to need it on a mountain in Arizona.

Once everything was packed the two young men got

into the small SUV and headed out from their long term home in Amarillo. They both planned on returning, they both expected this to be a few weeks to a few months adventure, but as the car pulled out of the parking spot they both felt the change in their world. Some part of each one of them knew their life was changing at that moment, they hoped it was for the better, they hoped it was the last time they would have to think about money. No matter what it was they were both committed to following through whether that meant wandering around Arizona until they found nothing or if it meant climbing a mountain into the sky and facing a hoard of vicious animals that were summoned by an ancient creator, they were both ready and willing to let their lives change.